Hi, I'm JIMMY!

Like me, you probably noticed the world is run by adults.
But ask yourself: Who would do the best job
of making books that *kids* will love?

Yeah. **Kids!**

So that's how the idea of JIMMY books came to life.
We want every JIMMY book to be so good
that when you're finished, you'll say,

"PLEASE GIVE ME ANOTHER BOOK!"

Give this one a try and see if you agree.
(If not, you're probably an adult!)

JIMMY PATTERSON BOOKS
FOR YOUNG READERS

James Patterson Presents

Sci-Fi Junior High by John Martin and Scott Seegert

Sci-Fi Junior High: Crash Landing by John Martin and Scott Seegert

How to Be a Supervillain by Michael Fry

How to Be a Supervillain: Born to Be Good by Michael Fry

The Unflushables by Ron Bates

The Middle School Series by James Patterson

Middle School: The Worst Years of My Life

Middle School: Get Me Out of Here!

Middle School: Big Fat Liar

Middle School: How I Survived Bullies, Broccoli, and Snake Hill

Middle School: Ultimate Showdown

Middle School: Save Rafe!

Middle School: Just My Rotten Luck

Middle School: Dog's Best Friend

Middle School: Escape to Australia

Middle School: From Hero to Zero

The I Funny Series by James Patterson

I Funny

I Even Funnier

I Totally Funniest

I Funny TV

I Funny: School of Laughs

I Funny: Around the World

The Treasure Hunters Series by James Patterson

Treasure Hunters

Treasure Hunters: Danger Down the Nile

For exclusives, trailers, and other information,
visit jamespatterson.com.

THE UNFLUSHABLES

RON BATES

JIMMY Patterson Books

LITTLE, BROWN AND COMPANY
New York Boston London

Copyright © 2018 by Ron Bates
Foreword © 2018 by James Patterson
Illustrations copyright © 2018 by Erin Hunting

Hachette Book Group supports the right to free expression and the value of copyright. The purpose of copyright is to encourage writers and artists to produce the creative works that enrich our culture.

The scanning, uploading, and distribution of this book without permission is a theft of the author's intellectual property. If you would like permission to use material from the book (other than for review purposes), please contact permissions@hbgusa.com. Thank you for your support of the author's rights.

JIMMY Patterson Books / Little, Brown and Company
Hachette Book Group
1290 Avenue of the Americas, New York, NY 10104
jamespatterson.com

First Edition: April 2018

JIMMY Patterson Books is an imprint of Little, Brown and Company, a division of Hachette Book Group, Inc. The Little, Brown name and logo are trademarks of Hachette Book Group, Inc. The JIMMY Patterson Books® name and logo are trademarks of JBP Business, LLC.

The publisher is not responsible for websites (or their content) that are not owned by the publisher.

The Hachette Speakers Bureau provides a wide range of authors for speaking events. To find out more, go to hachettespeakersbureau.com or call (866) 376-6591.

Library of Congress Cataloging-in-Publication Data
Names: Bates, Ron, author.
Title: The unflushables / Ron Bates.
Description: First edition. | New York : JIMMY Patterson Books, Little, Brown and Company, 2018. | Summary: Thirteen-year-old Sully Stringfellow, his arch-nemesis Izzy Cisco, friend Moleman, and a league of long-forgotten plumber heroes team up to save Nitro City from mutant creatures in the sewers.
Identifiers: LCCN 2017032394 | ISBN 978-0-316-51000-4
Subjects: | CYAC: Plumbers—Fiction. | Heroes—Fiction. | Monsters—Fiction. | Underground areas—Fiction. | Middle schools—Fiction. | Schools—Fiction. | Humorous stories.
Classification: LCC PZ7.B671675 Unf 2018 | DDC [Fic]—dc23
LC record available at https://lccn.loc.gov/2017032394.

10 9 8 7 6 5 4 3 2 1

LSC-C

Printed in the United States of America

To Thomas Crapper
1836–1910
Plumber. Inventor. Punch line.
Thanks for being a good sport about it.

Foreword

Why did the superhero flush the toilet?

Because it was his doody.

HA! If you laughed at that joke, twelve-year-old me would've given you a high five. I've always loved potty humor—that's why I just had to publish *The Unflushables*. In the wacky town of Nitro City, the plumbers are the true superheroes. And it's their *doody* to fight mutant sewer creatures, like the croctopus and mucus monsters, and keep them from taking over the city. This book reminds me of some of my favorite stories, with awesome action scenes and hilarious, gross-out jokes like in *Teenage Mutant Ninja Turtles* and *Ghostbusters*. I ain't afraid of no jokes!

—James Patterson

Chapter 1

He who controls the sewers controls everything.

The Greeks knew it.
The Romans knew it. Now you know it.

Monday, 1:34 p.m.

I'm a tiger, still and silent, waiting to pounce. That's what I keep telling myself. It might be easier to believe if this were a jungle instead of the third stall in the downstairs boys' restroom, but I go where the trail leads me. I'm hunkered down, gripping my knees for warmth. Why is it so cold in here? Probably because there's a weird hissing toilet poking me in the backbone. What do they make those things out of, ice? It doesn't matter. Right now, I'm only thinking about three things:

Who's it going to be?

When's it going to happen?

What did I just step in?

I'm not going to lie, that last one worries me a lot. I mean, I've seen Timmy Wattenberger use this stall. No offense, but I play basketball with Timmy—he can't hit the rim. Just thinking about his terrible aim gives me the willies. I'm tempted to scoot away, but a sound stops me...

Footsteps.

Not ordinary footsteps—heavy, trudging thuds like someone has given a musk ox a hall pass. The restroom door glides open, then slowly closes again. I take a deep breath, count to ten, and burst out of the stall like a claustrophobic rodeo bull.

"Hello, Mumford."

Mumford Milligan lets out a high, piercing, baby-like squeal. It's embarrassing for both of us.

"Wh—what the..." he shrieks. "Are you stupid or something? You coulda gave me a heart attack!"

Please. We both know Mumford has no heart.

"What are you doing in here, Mumford?"

I'll be honest, it's not a great question to ask in the

bathroom. But someone in this school has been clogging toilets, and I don't have time for niceties.

"Nuthin'," he grunts.

It's the answer I expected, just not the one I want.

"So what have you got behind you?"

"What…this?" he says.

He pulls his hand out from behind his back, and it's
like he's surprised to find there's a cigarette in it. But
I'm not. My nose picked up that noxious death-stick
the second he lit it up.

"It's not mine," he lies. "I, uh, found it. It was in the
hall. I just came in here to get rid of it."

"Oh? You mean like you got rid of these?"

I show him the plastic bag I have in my pocket.
Inside it is an ugly, mangled, moldy wad of partially
decomposed bathroom-butts.

"I pulled these out this morning," I tell him. "They
get stuck in the pipe."

Mumford looks like he might be sick.

"You mean you got those out of the toilet?" he asks.

I nod.

"And you carry them around in a little bag?"

Oh, sure, leave it to Mumford to turn this into

something weird. Do I like having half-flushed toilet tobacco in my pocket? No. But there's a Phantom Clogger out there, and I'm going to find him.

Unfortunately, it's not Mumford. I can see that now. Mumford's smoking some cheap, flimsy stink-log. The Phantom? He goes for the fancy stuff—Torpedoes. I know because I've found them at the scene of every clog. They're his signature brand.

Which means I'm wasting my time.

"Just keep your lip-warmers out of my toilets," I growl.

It's probably not the smartest thing I could've said. I mean, first of all, they're not "my" toilets. If they were, Timmy Wattenberger would never be allowed near them. And second of all, it's pretty clear I've been doing some unauthorized plumbing in here, which makes threatening Mumford a dangerous game. The fact is, if he wants to get me in trouble, he can. Big trouble. But he won't. Guys like Mumford don't turn in people like me—they have other ways of handling their problems.

Did I mention Mumford is enormous? He's a big, bulky eighth-grader with arms like jackhammers and a personality that ought to come with a warning label. I see an unsettling grin cross his face as he moves calmly to the nearest bowl and dangles the putrid puffer out over the rim, daring me to stop him. Am I scared?

Plenty. But I knew the risks when I walked into a middle school john.

I give him my fiercest glare, narrowing my eyes until they're squinty and hard. He gives one back to me. His looks tougher. Doesn't matter, it's too late to back off now. We're locked in a good old-fashioned bathroom stare-down, and neither of us wants to be the first to blink. It's only been a few seconds but my corneas already feel like walnut shells. The tension is unbearable. Suddenly, Mumford's hand twitches, I see his fingers move, and then…

He pulls the choker away from the bowl.

I can't believe it—he backed down. Quietly, I let myself start breathing again. But just when I think I'm out of the woods, Mumford flicks off the ashes, wads the cigarette into a ball—and swallows it.

"The next time I get rid of a butt, it's going to be yours," he says.

Then without another word, he turns and walks out the door.

It's over. Did I win?

Well, the Phantom Clogger is still out there, I just made Mumford Milligan's hit list, and my sneakers smell like somebody else's pee.

You tell me.

I rush down the hall toward Mr. Dunn's algebra class. Sure, he'll give me the stink-eye for being late, but I'm riding the line between a C and a B-minus, and if I fall any further behind—

The loudspeaker on the wall crackles.

"Sully Stringfellow, report to the principal's office. Sully Stringfellow to the principal's office."

Oh, well. When was I ever going to use algebra, anyway?

Chapter 2

Monday, 2:12 p.m.

I walk into the principal's office, which is a small, crowded room inside a bigger, crowded room near the front of the school building. The principal is sitting in a high-back chair turned to the window. He swivels to face me.

"Sully," he says.

"Leonard," I answer, collapsing into the green armchair across from him. I grab an orange jelly bean from the big jar on his desk and pop it into my mouth.

It's our standard routine.

"I'll tell you why I called you here," he says.

"Toilet in the downstairs boys' room? Third stall?"

He looks surprised.

"Yes. How did you know?"

"It's a troublemaker," I tell him. "I've had my eye on it for a while, but I've been a little busy with—"

"The Phantom Clogger?"

I nod. "He's still out there—and up to his old tricks."

Leonard's normally blank face develops deep worry lines. He jumps to his feet and leans over his desk.

"He's got to be stopped, Sully. I put you on this job because I thought you could get results!"

"I'm trying!" I say.

"Well, try harder. I can't keep having toilets go down, not with this many students. It's bad enough that I have to worry about..."

He doesn't finish his thought. Instead, his voice trails off like someone who's said too much already.

"What's wrong?" I ask.

The anger leaves Leonard's face, and in no time, he's back to looking like a potato with glasses.

"I know what you think, Sully," he says. "You think a principal's job is all about power, and detentions, and telling people what to do. But that's just the fun part. The truth is, my day is filled with more responsibilities than you can imagine. And it all starts in the bathroom."

"The bathroom?"

His eyes flash and he points a long, skinny finger at me.

"A school without a functioning bathroom is not a school—it's chaos!" he says. "Look, I haven't told you this, but the Phantom Clogger isn't our biggest problem. Sinks, water fountains, the showers in the gym— they're all slowing down. It'd be one thing if it was just happening here, but it's not. I've talked to other principals, and this is system-wide. And last week at Nitro High…they found something in one of the toilets."

The tension in the room is as thick as extra-chunky peanut butter.

"Was it…" I ask, almost afraid to finish the question, "big?"

Leonard bites his bottom lip and nods.

"It wasn't a student who found it, thank goodness," he says. "They were able to call someone who could handle it quietly before anyone found out."

When Leonard says "anyone," he means Ironwater.

They're the corporation that controls the plumbing in Nitro City. According to them, the pipes in the schools are absolutely, 100 percent fail-proof. They're not, of course, which is why when something goes wrong, they blame the principal.

No wonder Leonard looks worried.

"These are troubled times, Sully. You don't know half of what's going on," he says. "I need every stall open for business, and I need it by tomorrow."

"Tomorrow? Why tomorrow?"

Leonard turns toward the window and puts his hands in his pockets. He lets out a long, troubled sigh.

"Tomorrow is Tuesday, Sully. Taco Tuesday."

I gulp. At Gloomy Valley Middle School, the second Tuesday of every month is half-price tacos in the cafeteria. They're very popular.

"I'm sorry. I forgot," I say.

Leonard shakes his head.

"You're not the one who put them on the menu. So...can you help me?"

"Can you get me out of PE?"

"That's your fifth period, right?"

"Right," I say.

"I'll write you a hall pass."

Of course he will. Leonard—or Principal Bogart, which is what I have to call him everywhere except in this office—knows how to get things done. He's a practical guy—I could tell it the minute I saw his buzz haircut, clip-on tie, and no-nonsense loafers. We've got a sweet little arrangement, him and me: Leonard gets his drains fixed without attracting any attention, and I get a day away from the athletic torture chamber known as physical education.

Of course, if Ironwater ever found out I was messing with the plumbing system...well, let's just hope that never happens.

Leonard hands me the pass, meaning our business is done. I stuff it in my pocket and start toward the door.

"Sully," he calls out after me. "The Phantom Clogger?"

My eyes narrow and I feel my jaw clench.

"Don't worry, Leonard," I tell him. "I'll flush him out."

Chapter 3

Monday, 10:08 p.m.

"Creepy crawlers in your pipe—
Make you want to fuss and gripe—
Don't let creatures spoil your day—
Use Muta-Nix—and then flush away!"

"Muta-Nix is the number one anti-mutation treatment on the market. Use it once a week to keep your drains clean, shiny, and mutant-free! That's Muta-Nix, a division of Ironwater."

5...4...3...2...1...aaaaaaaaaaand my door opens. Great. Here we go again.

"It's after ten. What'd I tell you about that TV?"

"The TV's not on, Big Joe. It was my computer."

"Computer? They've got commercials on the computer?"

I nod, but I'm not sure he believes me.

"They pop up on the internet. It's kind of annoying."

I only mention that last part because being annoyed is one of Joe's hobbies. He gets grouchier before breakfast than most people do all day.

"Noise is noise," he says, forming his mouth into an upside-down horseshoe. "I don't want to hear it after ten."

I nod again and hope that's the end of it, but he's still looking at me. Is he mad? I honestly can't tell. That's the problem with living with an old grump—they always look mad. I'm trying to remember whether he looked this grumpy before—maybe, but I don't think so. I do know that except for the permanent frown, he looks exactly the same as he did when I was little: large head, no neck, thick chest, thicker belly, and a pair of khaki pants that keeps falling down in the back.

Big Joe Feeney is my grandfather, so it's not like I'm sharing a house with a complete stranger, but it's close. He disappeared four years ago without saying a word to anybody. I didn't even know he was back in town until three months ago—that's when I moved in here. It was the only place I could go after I lost my parents.

Okay, I didn't actually lose them—I mean, I know what ocean they're in. They're on Viti Levu, which is in the Fiji Islands, which are in the Pacific Ocean, which is on planet Earth, or at least that's what they keep telling me. I guess I'm supposed to find it reassuring that if I really need them, they're just a hop, skip, and 7,933 miles away. I mean, it's not as if they abandoned me and went to Mars, which would have been irresponsible and kind of awesome. No, the way they tell it, they're still right down the hall like they've always been, but now our house is the size of the Western Hemisphere.

"Honey, this is a good thing for all of us. Especially you," my mom said when she sprang the news about my abandonment. "Yes, I'm being transferred to Fiji, and your dad and your sister are coming with me, but you...you're going to have your own amazing adventure right here!"

An adventure? Oh boy! What skinny, defenseless thirteen-year-old wouldn't love being left alone in Nitro City, the most dangerous place on Earth?

All right, technically Nitro City is "The Most EXPLOSIVE Place on Earth," at least according to the billboard at the edge of town. That's supposed to mean we have a "booming" population, but everyone knows it's because there used to be a nitroglycerin factory here. It blew up decades ago, and the chemicals seeped into the ground, and some people say that's what started all the weirdness. Me? I don't know. I think some places are just naturally weird.

Some *people*, too.

What's he doing over there? He's just staring at a wall. Is this still about the noise?

"What is this?" Joe says.

"That's a poster, Big Joe."

"You just put this up?"

"Yeah. Today."

"Hmmmmm…"

Okay, now I'm lost. Is he frowning or is he thinking? Big Joe is a hard one to read. He runs his hand through that thick mop of gray hair and walks the length of the wall.

"Seems like you've got a lot of these," he says.

"Not really. I know people with more."

"There are people with more stuff like this?"

He's stopped in front of a faded black-and-white poster of Tank Huberman.

"Not exactly like that one. It's vintage."

"Vintage?" he says. "That mean ugly?"

Ugly? Tank Huberman isn't ugly. He just has what we call plumber's face.

"It means old," I tell him.

I don't know the exact date, but that particular picture is from at least thirty years ago. And it's a classic, the one where Tank is covered in dirt and bruises, and both eyes are nearly swollen shut. At the top of the poster, in big white letters, are the words THE TANK, because that's what everyone called him. It's an original, not a reprint like some of my friends have. I'm kind of a collector, I guess, but only stuff from plumbing's Golden Age. I've got Tank Huberman, Snake Johnson, Captain Clog, the Pipe Princess—some of the really big names.

"Bunch of old junk," Big Joe says.

His voice sounds strange, almost like he's talking to the posters instead of to me. I'm not going to lie—I'm a little creeped out.

"You don't think these guys were great?"

Joe stares at the wall, taking in the pictures one at a time.

"Who remembers?" he says.

He looks back at the Tank Huberman poster.

"You know this one went to jail, right?"

I nod.

"That doesn't bother you?"

"What do you mean?" I ask him.

"Waking up every morning face-to-face with a criminal. You're okay with that?"

I'd never thought about it that way—having a criminal on my wall. But I know quite a bit about the Tank, what he was before everything changed, and what he became after. And yeah, I'm okay with it.

"He didn't do anything really bad," I tell him. "He was just plumbing, the same as he did when it was legal. It's not like he was the Midnight Flush or something."

Joe starts to answer, then rolls his eyes. He's in one of his moods. I could argue with him, but what's the point? It's not like he'd listen.

"What time are you coming home tomorrow?" he says.

"Probably late. School lets out at three thirty, but I'm going straight to work."

I wait, sure that he's going to ask me about my after-school job, but he doesn't. He's never asked about it—not once. I used to think that was odd, but considering the way he just glared at my walls, I hope he never does.

Chapter 4

Tuesday, 5:14 p.m.

Gladys looks angry, which is how most people look when they see us. She's standing in the doorway with her arms crossed like some genie that only grants horrible wishes.

"Are you the..." she says, then looks around and lowers her voice to a whisper, "plumber?"

We nod.

"You were supposed to be here two hours ago!"

"And you were supposed to be charming," says

Max, walking right past her into the house. "It's been a disappointing day for both of us."

Gladys's mouth opens so wide I could perform dental surgery.

I call her "Gladys" because she looks like a Gladys, meaning she's short and squatty with big, shiny doll eyes and hair the color of Velveeta cheese. I like to give the customers made-up names, since most of them don't bother to introduce themselves. Probably because they're hoping to never see us again.

"Thisssss way," Gladys hisses.

We walk into the master bedroom and stop in front of a plain brown door. Max grabs the plastic doorknob that, for some reason, looks like a gaudy plastic diamond.

"You might want to stand back, lady," he says.

Then he gives me the "go" sign, I give it back, and we move in.

That's when I see them—those scaly, bug-eyed creatures we'd encountered in far too many bathrooms. Glaring at us from every wall are dozens of decorative ceramic clown fish.

"Don't freak out," Max warns me.

"They watch me when I pee," I whisper.

Which is true. Why people put these things in their homes is one of the great mysteries of our age. I'm focusing on a disturbingly large specimen hanging just above the medicine cabinet when something else catches my attention.

It's the toilet lid whizzing past my head.

I turn just in time to see a horde of giant mutant tentacles bursting out of the bowl.

"Croctopus!" I shout, and leap back into the bedroom.

If you've never seen a croctopus, they're easy enough to identify—enormous crocodile jaws, flailing octopus-like tentacles, a smell that makes you want to have your nostrils removed...

Max hits the deck and tuck-rolls across the floor while the beast's slimy feelers lash at him like bull-whips. He reaches the corner behind the sink, springs to his feet, and flattens his back against the wall.

"Okay, I think I found the trouble," he says. "Looks like you've got a blockage in your sewer line. Big job."

Gladys's doll eyes pop wide open. "How big?"

He shoots her his million-dollar grin, which, if I know Max, will be included in the final bill.

Max Bleeker can be an intimidating guy. He's six

three, taller if you count that bright-red tower he calls a flattop. He wears black boots and sunglasses. His tight-fitting T-shirt makes his biceps look like over-inflated party balloons. But once you get past the rudeness, the selfish behavior, and the bad disposition, you'll find he's genuinely unpleasant to be around.

"P.C.," he says, snapping his fingers.

I should explain that when Max says P.C., it means he wants his plunger caddy. And by plunger caddy, I mean me. That's my job—carrying the plunger—which isn't nearly as glamorous as it sounds. Personally, I would've preferred a title like "wrench valet" or "vice president in charge of tool distribution," but no one asked my opinion.

I cross the room and—very gently—extend a clipboard through the web of flapping tentacles. Max scribbles a number on the page and hands it back to me. I show it to Gladys.

"For a clogged toilet?" she shrieks. "Look, if you think I'm going to pay this much, then—"

"Oh, for cryin' out loud, just shut up and write the check!"

I'm stunned. While this is exactly the kind of thing I'd expect Max to say, it wasn't Max who said it. It was a completely different voice—and it was coming from inside the bathroom. Carefully, I look through the doorway and spot a soap-covered, middle-aged man peeking out from behind the shower curtain.

Gladys rolls her eyes.

"That's my husband, Bud," she says. "He was in the shower when one of those leg-thingies started flopping out of the john this morning. Then it was, 'Call somebody! Call somebody!'"

"Just pay the man!" Bud screams.

"Oh, all right!"

Gladys glares at Max, then pulls a checkbook from her pocket and appears to be trying to stab it to death with her pen. I can't blame her for being upset. It's a big number. Still, it's a bargain compared to what she would've had to pay Ironwater—and she knows it.

I mean, isn't that why she called an outlaw plumber in the first place?

When Gladys finally finishes murdering our payment, she hands it to me and I take it to Max. He stuffs it in his jeans, flips his Ray-Bans back down over his eyes, and turns toward the creature.

"Okay, beautiful," he says. "Let's dance."

From my spot at the doorway, I watch a pair of

black, unblinking lizard eyes slowly rise out of the smooth white bowl. I don't mind telling you it is the single grossest thing I have ever seen in a toilet, and I go to public school. The green snout climbs higher and higher while the twitching tentacles flow across the floor like melting ice.

Reaching into the big blue duffel, I pull out a long-handled, thirty-six-inch pipe wrench and hand it to Max. He grabs hold of the heavy titanium handle, adjusts the gripping jaw, and—*WHAP!*—whacks the bejeezus out of a wriggling limb.

Yellow pus splatters the fish-lined walls.

"He's a maniac!" Bud screams, then races into the bedroom, the shower curtain streaming behind him like a Superman cape.

Max pays no attention. He swings again, opening a deep gash in the creature's squirmy flesh. Suddenly, a tentacle bursts through the side of the bowl and wraps itself around his waist, flinging him hard against the doorjamb. He grunts painfully, then looks at Gladys.

"You're also going to need a new...toilet," he tells her. "That's extra!"

The words are barely out of his mouth before the monster lifts him into the air and smashes him against the ceiling. He drops the wrench. I lunge for it, but just as my fingers reach the handle, something wet and slimy slithers up my leg. The next thing I know, a thick green tentacle is dragging me across the floor. I claw at the tiles, but there's nothing to hold on to, nothing to—

Wait a minute…what is that? My hand brushes against something cold and smooth—and sharp. It's porcelain, a jagged chunk from the broken toilet. I snatch it like it's the last slice of pizza at a sleepover party, and plunge it into the horrible limb.

The creature's scream sounds like a thousand cats fighting over the same ball of yarn. It loosens its hold, and I scramble to my feet. Tentacles chasing after me, I make a mad, desperate leap back into the bedroom.

"Now!" Max yells.

I shove my arm into the duffel and pull out what I instinctively know he wants—a drain-grenade. In one fluid motion, I pull the pin and throw the small black clog-remover to Max. He catches it in his hand, then rockets it down the hideous, hollow throat of the octo-freak.

"3…2…1…"

KA-BLAAAAAAAM!

For the next several seconds, there's a high-pitched

ringing in my ears, and then everything goes quiet. When I peek around the corner, I see that the toilet has vanished. There's water streaming from a broken pipe, and all four walls are painted in gooey, roasted mutant guts. Slowly, Max emerges from the smoldering remains of what used to be the master bathroom. He pauses in the doorway, raises a can of pine-scented air freshener—and sprays.

"You're not going to want to go in there for a while," he says.

Chapter 5

Wednesday, 9:38 a.m.

"All right, people. Today we're going to be discussing the history of the mutant outbreak. But before we get started, I'd like to—"

The door to the classroom slowly creaks open. Mrs. Gladwell turns her head like an owl looking for prey.

"You're late, Nixon."

"Sorry, Mrs. Gladwell. There was a line in the bathroom."

"Again?" she tells him. "All right, then, just don't let it—"

"I mean, a long line. The kind you see for a roller coaster at Six Flags," he says. "I wouldn't have waited, but it was an emergency."

"Yes, Nixon, I see. Now if you'll—"

"A big emergency," he continues. "My stomach was already making that noise, the one that sounds like air shooting out of a wet balloon."

"I understand. Now please—"

"It was embarrassing. No one wanted to stand next to me in line. I think it might have been something I ate. Does bologna go bad?"

"Nixon!" Mrs. Gladwell yells, and the room falls stone silent. She pauses a second, then smooths back her short gray hair. "It's fine, Nixon. I understand that you were tardy because you had a more pressing... obligation."

"Oh, it wasn't an obligation," he says. "It was a doody."

I bust out laughing, and before long, the whole class loses it. Mumford Milligan nearly falls out of his seat.

"Just sit down, Nixon," Mrs. Gladwell sighs.

He takes his place in the desk next to mine.

"Nice," I whisper.

He shrugs.

"I thought I could keep it going longer, but she cut me off. Oh, well, next time."

Nixon Funk is an interesting kid. He looks permanently sleepy, like a depressed walrus, and he combs his hair into thin brown bangs that come halfway down his forehead. He's got one of those in-between-sized bodies—the kind they call "husky" if you're an athlete, and "chunky" if you're not. Nixon is not. He also has the sharpest tongue, fastest comebacks, and most annoying self-confidence I have ever seen in a thirteen-year-old.

On two occasions, I have watched him make teachers cry. It wouldn't surprise me if he ends up expelled, or in prison, or ruling the world, because that's what happens to people like Nixon.

I probably wouldn't have anything to do with him if he wasn't my best friend. But he is.

"Is that true about the bathroom having a line?" I ask him.

"Yeah. Everybody has to use the one upstairs because the downstairs one is broken again. They blocked the door with yellow tape and everything. Looks like a crime scene over there."

Crime scene? The Phantom? No, I would've

heard something by now. Still, this is the third major plumbing breakdown this week. Something weird is happening, something that goes way beyond ordinary clogs. I just wish I knew what it was.

"As I was saying," Mrs. Gladwell starts over, her eyes landing hard on Nixon, "we'll be discussing the mutant outbreak and its effect on society. But first, I want you to watch something."

She rolls a TV to the front of the room and turns out the lights. After a couple of seconds, little black-and-white specks flicker across the screen, which means whatever we're watching is ancient. When the specks vanish, there's some terrible music, then a blurry old message appears.

The American Plumbing Institute Presents:
YOUR BATHROOM AND YOU

Suddenly, the scene changes and we're looking at a cartoon toilet.

"This is John," the announcer tells us. *"John is like a member of the family. He lives with you in your house, and he's there for you day or night. So you can always trust John whenever you go for a visit, right?*

"WRONG!

"*Even though John is a good friend, he should never be trusted! Because under John's lid lurks a menace more dangerous than cigarettes and communism combined. And that danger is...STOOL!*

"*Yes, S.T.O.O.L.*

"**S***ewage*

"**T***ransformed*

"**O***versized*

"**O***ddities and*

"**L***ife-forms.*

"*These mutated creatures crawl through pipes and drains, turning even the friendliest John into a perilous potty of doom!*

"*So if you see something scary inside your toilet bowl, what should you do?*

"*CALL A PLUMBER!*

"*American plumbers are the heroes of our age. They unstop our sinks and do courageous battle against the evil that dwells below. You can feel safe knowing they'll be there, now and in the future, doing those jobs too tough for robots and the atomic bomb.*

"*The American Plumber! Bonded. Certified. Licensed to Kill.*"

THE END

The classroom lights come back on.

"What in the freakin' fudge cake was that?" Mumford asks.

"It's a safety film," Mrs. Gladwell says. "They used to show it to elementary school students to teach them how to handle a plumbing emergency. This was in the early days before we had anti-mutant technology. Back then, it wasn't unusual for someone to walk into their bathroom and find a sewer monster waiting in their toilet."

I've got news for her—it's not unusual now. I mean, it's not an everyday thing like it was during the Golden Age, but it's definitely not rare. People just think it is because nobody talks about it.

Not if they know what's good for them.

"Anti-mutant technology changed everything," Mrs. Gladwell says. "Without it, Nitro City would've been completely defenseless."

Defenseless? My hand is up in a flash.

"What about P.L.U.N.G.E.?" I ask.

"P.L.U.N.G.E.?"

"The Plumbers' League of—"

"I know what P.L.U.N.G.E. is, Sully. I just don't see what they have to do with this discussion."

P.L.U.N.G.E., the Plumbers' League of UnNaturally Gifted Exceptionals, were the most amazing plumbers the world has ever seen. Even before the mutant outbreak, they were the guardians of the sewer, defending it against some of the evilest names on the planet. Thaddeus Sludge, Dr. Toxic, Sal Monella, the Human Waste—they all tried to take over the Underworld. P.L.U.N.G.E. stopped them.

As far as I'm concerned, that makes them part of any discussion.

Izzy Cisco's hand shoots into the air.

"Mrs. Gladwell, isn't it true that P.L.U.N.G.E. was a danger to the community?" she asks.

"That's correct, Izzy."

"And if someone had actually read their homework assignment, wouldn't they know that's the reason the city made it illegal for them to be plumbers anymore?"

I notice Izzy isn't looking at Mrs. Gladwell. She's looking at me. And smiling. It's a stuck-up, taunting, vicious smile, because it comes from her soul.

"For your information, I *did* read the homework!" I snap. "Did you watch the movie? Because the movie said plumbers were heroes."

Mrs. Gladwell walks back to the TV screen, which is still showing a cartoon toilet.

"That's a good point, Sully. But remember, this film was made during plumbing's 'Golden Age,'" she says. "In those days, people did treat plumbers like heroes. You'd see their pictures on magazine covers, posters, cereal boxes—everywhere. The public was scared, and P.L.U.N.G.E. was very effective in pushing back the mutants. But in the process, they turned the city into a war zone. Their methods caused enormous damage. That's why, in the end, the city council handed all plumbing services over to a single corporation. Can anyone tell me the name?"

A dozen hands go up, but Mrs. Gladwell ignores them.

"What about you, Sully?"

I stare at her for a second, then grit my teeth.

"Ironwater," I mumble.

Man, I wish I could spit. Just saying the word leaves a bad taste in my mouth.

Chapter 6

Wednesday, 3:52 p.m.

When I get home, I walk into the den and find it empty—well, sort of empty. Big Joe's creepy recliner is in here. I say "creepy" because the leather cushions are formed into a lifelike mold of Joe's body. It's permanently cemented in front of the TV.

"...so it looks like those storm clouds are jusssssst going to miss us, and we can expect mild temperatures and no rain the rest of the week," Doppler Doug, the Channel 6 weatherman, says. "Which is good news for anyone with outdoor plans this weekend."

"But bad news if you're an umbrella salesman, Doppler Doug," Channel 6 news anchor Pepper Hayes says back.

I like watching the news on Channel 6 because the people there are always happy. It's like they don't know they're telling us terrible things.

"Turning to local news, there was a big mess in Nitro City today when an auxiliary sewage pipe exploded inside the central wastewater-treatment plant," Pepper says with a smile. "Sabotage is suspected."

Suddenly, Pepper vanishes from the screen, and I'm looking at a chubby, thick-necked man who doesn't seem happy at all. He has beady eyes, and very little hair, and a button that says VOTE FOR TODD.

"As you know, Ironwater is this city's only authorized plumbing services provider," Harlon Todd, the city's mayor, says, "and I'm committed to giving them the resources they need to protect our drains and pipelines from those who would do them harm. So, remember, on election day, vote for Todd—the only candidate who will put your tax dollars into the sewer!"

The TV screen flickers for a second and then Pepper is back, and just like that, the world feels sunny again.

"Ironwater chairman Herman Wiest blamed the blast on rebel plumbers headed by the Midnight Flush," she says. "No one was injured, but toilets were backed up across the city."

Man, those rebel plumbers have been busy lately. It seems like every other day they're hitting something— a sewer line, a pumping station, a water main. It's been all over the news. What I don't understand is how they got into a wastewater-treatment plant in the first place. Those things are guarded like fortresses. And even if they got inside, how could they—

CLI-ICK.

I hear a noise behind me and see Big Joe coming in from the garage. He doesn't say hello, because Joe is allergic to common courtesy, but he gives me a quick look as he heads for the front door.

"Come on," he says.

"Where are we going?"

"Work. I got a call about a repair job over on Third Street. You're going to help me with it. That all right?"

I nod, but even as my head bobs up and down, I'm trying to think of an excuse to get out of it. This is terrible—I don't want to work with Big Joe. And why would he want me to? We deliberately live in two different parts of the house just to keep from spending time together. Is this some sort of punishment?

I close my eyes and try to tell myself it won't be so bad.

Oh, who am I kidding? It's already bad! Just look at the way he's staring at me. It's the way a wolf stares at a sheep who just agreed to help him go do wolf stuff.

I lower my head and make the slow, sad walk out to the truck.

Chapter 7

Big Joe pulls up in front of a ritzy old building on Third Street, and a chill runs up my spine. That usually means there's something dark and evil nearby, but maybe I'm just freaked out by all the monsters.

Because there's a lot of them.

Not real monsters. Gargoyles. But even in statue form, they're the creepiest thing since nose hair. They're everywhere, perched up on the ledges of the building like a flock of hideous stone pigeons. What kind of a person wants to live in a place that's covered in little demon-faced dragon monsters? Probably someone deeply disturbed.

We head to the sixth floor, and I ring the bell. A tall, dark-haired girl in a black T-shirt with a big skull on it answers the door. The chill in my spine turns to ice.

"You!" I say.

It's Izzy Cisco—my nemesis!

"What do you want, sewer boy?" she says, frowning so much I think her face is melting.

Big Joe steps in front of me.

"Hello, young lady. We're here about the repair job."

Izzy smiles at him.

"Mom! There's a nice man and his helper monkey here to fix the wall!"

I'm about to unleash a scorching counter-burn when Joe shoves me through the door. After that, I'm too stunned to respond. Because, wow, the place is a palace—marble floors, arched doorways, furniture that looks like it came out of a magazine…

I never pictured Izzy Cisco living in a place like this. I thought she'd be out on the ledge with the other horrible creatures.

"Nice place," I tell her.

"What's so nice about it?"

"Everything but you."

Izzy rolls her eyes and walks past me like I'm nothing. A second later she plunks down on a cushy white couch and disappears behind a book called *Kiss of the Vampire*.

"Watch it," Big Joe tells me.

Watch what? Can I help it if Izzy Cisco doesn't like me? I'm pretty sure Izzy Cisco doesn't like anybody.

Suddenly, a slim woman appears in the hallway. She's wearing a tan button-down shirt with white pants. Her fingernails match the highlights in her hair.

"Hi, I'm Kate Cisco," she says. "Sorry to keep you waiting."

Mrs. Cisco has big, dark eyes and a friendly smile. It's like looking at an older, non-horrible version of Izzy. We follow her down the hall and stop at the master bathroom.

"I want to replace the baseboards in here," she says. "And I'd also like to do something about the trim."

She lists a few other things, but to be honest, I'm not paying attention. How can I? I'm just a few feet away from the most heavenly shower ever connected to a mortal bathroom. Five showerheads, gold fixtures, marble tile…

"Awesome shower," I blurt out.

"Oh...thank you," Mrs. Cisco says. "I just wish it worked."

"It doesn't?"

I hear a growl, but I can't tell if it's coming from Joe's face or his stomach. Either way, it sounds angry.

Mrs. Cisco shakes her head. "The drain keeps backing up. One day it's fine, the next day it's stopped up again," she explains, then drops her voice to a whisper. "And there's a smell."

Wait...Izzy has a smelly shower? This is big news and I have a million questions, but Joe's stare shuts me down.

"I think we can handle it from here, ma'am," he says.

Mrs. Cisco nods politely and leaves. When the door closes, Big Joe eyes me for a second, then picks up his circular saw. He frowns.

"I need another blade," he says. "I've got one out in the truck. Wait here."

"Okay. While you're gone, I can—"

"You can do nothing," he says.

"But..."

"I mean it. Don't do anything," he warns me, then walks out the door.

I let out a bored sigh and plop down on the

fancy-pants tile floor. It's cool, and white, and smooth, and I kind of want to slide around on it in my socks. But I don't because I'm a professional.

Grrrrg-bloop.

What's that? A weird gurgling noise is coming from the shower. I walk over to the clear-glass door and open it. Everything looks okay. I don't smell anything, either. Okay, maybe the slightest hint of lavender shampoo, but if that's what's bothering Izzy's mom, she doesn't deserve to have nostrils.

I bend all the way over until my face is next to the drain, and that's when I pick up just a trace of something—

CLAAAANG!

The drain cover flies off. Before I know what's happening, long, spaghetti-like tentacles explode through the hole and wrap themselves around my head! Instinctively, I lunge backward, but they tighten and force my face to the floor. I feel them squeezing me, cutting off the circulation to my brain. In a desperate move, I put my hands on the floor and do the longest, most painful push-up of my life. The tentacles stretch, and an instant later, my head is free. I rocket backward, collapsing against the shower wall.

But just when I think it's over, four small, smelly creatures crawl out of the drain.

They're disgusting. I mean really disgusting. They look like squishy bowling balls with party streamers for legs. I jump to my feet and try to run, but a web of spidery tentacles clutches my kneecaps. There's a sudden yank, and I go crashing against the side of a tall wooden cabinet, toppling it to the floor. The creatures swarm me like bees on a honey thief.

Quickly, I reach behind me and feel something cool and dangerous—Big Joe's hammer. I swing wild, but get lucky. The hammerhead connects with one of the jellybeasts, splattering it against the side of a laundry hamper.

"Sully! Sully!"

It's Big Joe. He's pounding on the bathroom door, but the overturned cabinet is wedged against it. Before I can say anything, a squish-monster attaches itself to my face. Ewwwwwww! It smells like the inside of a bait bucket. I pry it loose and fling the thing into the bathroom sink. Then I bring the hammer down.

Unfortunately, the face-sucker is as quick as it is ugly. It moves, and I whack the shiny chrome faucet instead, sending a tall stream of water gushing into the air. Okay, now I'm mad. Swatting like an insane carpenter, I chase down the three remaining creatures and herd them back into the shower.

The silver hammer is nothing but a blur as I take out two showerheads, some Italian tiles, and an innocent soap dish. I must have broken a couple of pipes, because water is flooding the bathroom floor. But the worst part is, everywhere I look, there are bouncing blobs and tentacles striking at me like snakes. I lose my balance and fall through the shower door, shattering it into a million pieces. My head hits the floor hard, and for an instant, everything goes black.

"Sully!"

That's weird…I can hear Big Joe on the other side of the door, but his voice seems strange and far away. In fact, everything seems far away. It's almost as if the world outside this room has disappeared, and nothing is left but me and the squishees. I don't know, maybe it's the fear, or the anger, or my possible concussion, but all of a sudden I feel different—like someone just flipped a switch and put my body on autopilot. Without thinking, I snatch a floating screwdriver out of the water and hurl it through the air. It spins a dozen times before nailing one of the blobs to the wall. I snag a second creature in a bath towel, and slingshot it against the ceiling. It bursts like a mucus-filled water balloon.

That means there's just one monster left—the one that's streaking right toward me. Moving on instinct, I roll out of the way, grab Mrs. Cisco's toilet plunger, and bat the thing like Babe Ruth hitting a homer. The blast knocks it against the back of the toilet, and it ricochets into the bowl.

Quickly, I slam down the lid, leap on top of it, and release an earsplitting victory cry.

A few seconds later, the overturned cabinet scoots across the wet tiles, and Big Joe and Mrs. Cisco come bursting through the door. I don't know what they're thinking, but I know what they see. They see spewing water pipes, broken fixtures, shattered glass, and a crazed thirteen-year-old standing on a toilet seat with a bath towel cape and a plunger raised up like the mighty sword Excalibur.

I can't imagine how this moment could be any more embarrassing...then Izzy appears in the doorway.

"Smile," she says.

Raising her phone, she points the camera at me, and clicks.

Chapter 8

Wednesday, 8:22 p.m.

Why isn't he screaming at me?

Those are the rules, right? If a kid screws up so bad it requires major home remodeling, he gets screamed at, or lectured, or, I don't know...something. It's the glue that holds society together. But here I am, stuck in the cab of a pickup with one of the all-time great hotheads, and he hasn't said a word. Not a single word. He hasn't even looked at me.

It's not human.

When we pull into the driveway, I'm out of the

truck before Big Joe even kills the engine. I don't know what he's planning, but I don't want to be near him when his hands come off the steering wheel. I rush into the house and head straight to my room. It takes a couple of minutes for the front door to open downstairs, but when it does, I brace myself for the slam... only it doesn't happen. Nothing happens.

I wish my mom was here. She would've had me grounded before I got off the toilet.

Of course, my mom isn't here. Neither is my dad. They're in Fiji with my little sister, and if you're wondering why I'm not with them, well, there's a good reason...

I'm a leak freak.

Don't like that one? How about plunger jockey? Flush puppy? Pooper trooper? Take your pick, I've heard them all. The bottom line is, I'm a born plumber, a freak of nature with a sump pump for a heart and copper pipes where my bones ought to be. Not literally, of course, but that would be awesome. All I know is that for as long as I can remember, I've been drawn to plumbing like a safecracker to a vault. I took my first sink apart when I was four. By six, I could reroute a sewer line. In another time and another place, they'd have called me a prodigy. But here?

I'm just the kid who's been kicked out of three middle schools in the past two years.

That's how I ended up at Gloomy Valley. See, it turns out most principals get very upset when you mess with school plumbing—at least mine did. But Leonard was different. Where the others saw a problem, he saw an opportunity. One that worked for both of us. Gloomy Valley is a long way from a perfect school, but it's a perfect fit for me.

Which explains why I'm not in Fiji. Once my parents finally found a middle school that was willing to let me stick around, they weren't about to rock the boat by moving me to the other side of the world.

I've got to be honest, the other side of the world is looking pretty good right now. I'm tired, filthy, and my body feels like a sea cow fell on it. I should probably eat something, but all I want to do is go to bed. I collapse on top of the covers, then reach over and grab the note from my dad I keep on my nightstand.

"Son, addresses are like underpants," it says. "Nobody likes to change the comfortable ones."

My dad is a poet, sometimes a great one. Just not lately. He kind of lost his confidence during a poetry competition when he couldn't come up with a rhyme for "purple." It's not his fault—everybody knows "purple" is the ultimate unrhymable word—but it still haunts him.

I miss my dad. I miss all of them. But there's nothing I can—

Creee-eeeek.

He's coming. There's no mistaking that groaning sound the wood makes as Big Joe moves up the stairs. I knew it wasn't over—he's just been toying with me, letting me twist in the wind. The door opens and I prepare myself for the stare-down of doom.

Only when Joe walks into the room, he doesn't even glance at me. He just strolls along my wall, studying the paper faces staring back at him.

"You look at these a lot, do you?" he asks.

"Yeah," I tell him.

He gives his head a slow shake and sighs.

"You're just like Teeny," he says. "She used to hang these things up all over the place."

"Mom put up plumber posters?"

"No, no," Joe says. "Rock bands. Bunch of weird-looking dudes with guitars. I didn't like the looks of 'em. Tattoos. Leather pants. I remember one of them had his tongue hanging out. I tore that one down, threw it away. I mean, I'm not going to have somebody sticking their tongue out at me in my own house. You gotta draw a line."

"Sure, I understand."

"Really?" he says, but I think he's only half listening. "Teeny never did."

For the record, my mom's name is Tina, which is a perfectly acceptable name for a grown woman. But to my knowledge, Big Joe has never used it. From the day she was born, he's called her Teeny, which means that from kindergarten through high school, she was known as Teeny Feeney.

I was starting to see why they didn't get along.

"Now, uh, about today," Joe says, and he looks down like he's trying to find the words on his feet. "There's something we need to discuss..."

I'll bet there is. I grit my teeth and wait for the verbal thrashing to begin.

"Your pay," he tells me.

My pay? I watch as Joe reaches into his wallet and pulls out a few bills.

"I know we didn't talk about an amount, but if you think this is fair…"

"Hold on…you want to pay me?"

He nods.

"For today?"

"I'm the one who took you on. I pay my crew," he says.

Oh, now I get it. Now I see exactly what's going on. This isn't about making me feel better—this is about making Joe look better. You see, if Joe doesn't pay me, then I was doing him a favor—which means he'll always be the guy who dragged his grandson to work and let him get attacked by squish monsters. But if he gives me money, then I'm just another employee—a stupid, bathroom-smashing employee he had the misfortune to get stuck with. And for a few bucks, he can be done with me.

Nice try, Joe. And to think I've been up here feeling guilty!

"No, thanks," I tell him.

"What?"

"I don't want your money, Joe. You keep it."

Big Joe looks surprised.

"You don't want to get paid?"

I shake my head.

"Well, you've got to want something."

"Just some sleep," I say. "I'm really tired."

Joe puts his wallet away, but he doesn't look happy about it. He's halfway out of the room when he stops to look at a poster of a dark-haired woman with an eye patch. She's swinging a pipe wrench.

"Now this one's not old," he says.

"That's One-Eyed Lily Cruz," I tell him. "She's not from the Golden Age. But she's an awesome plumber."

He squints his eyes for a closer look.

"Are those leather pants?"

Uh-oh. If Lily's tongue is hanging out, she's a goner.

Finally, Joe leaves, and two seconds later, my head hits the pillow. This has been one exhausting day. I'm just about to nod off when I hear footsteps coming back up the stairs. There's a muffled noise in the hallway. What's he doing out there? Slowly, I crawl out of bed, move toward the door, and open it. Big Joe is nowhere in sight, but there's a small box sitting on the floor.

Inside it, wrapped in a red rubber band, is a stack of old trading cards...*plumber* trading cards!

Chapter 9

Thursday, 11:44 a.m.

"That's Silky Lanier. *The* Silky Lanier!"

I nod but don't say anything, mostly because I'm playing it cool, but also because if I open my mouth even a little, I might squeal like a five-year-old on a pony ride. Nixon pushes the card back across the cafeteria table, and I whip out a few others. His jaw drops further and further as I show him Waterdog Jones, and Amber Waves, and the Mad Piper, and Drainiac McGee.

"*The* Drainiac McGee!" he gasps.

Nixon's excited, and why wouldn't he be? When I left school yesterday, I had an ordinary hand—now it's holding some of Nitro City's greatest treasures.

"So you wrecked a bathroom, and he gave you all these?"

"Not just these," I tell him.

I'm trying to fight back a grin, but it's tough because I've saved the best for last. I reach into my backpack and, nice and easy, pull out a standard 2½" x 3½" card. Nixon's eyes, which at their most alert are gopher-ish slits, grow to the size of donuts.

"No…way!" he screams. "The Midnight Flush?"

"Can you believe it?"

"What did he say?"

"Nothing."

"Nothing?"

"Nothing. I asked him about it this morning, but he just growled and ignored me."

"Why would anybody give up the Midnight Flush?"

"I don't know. I think he might be insane."

"I wish my grandfather was insane," Nixon says. "Wow, the Midnight Flush!"

If you know anything about plumbing, you know that the Midnight Flush is a really rare card, but it's more than that—the Midnight Flush is a forbidden card. They pulled them off the market when Ironwater named him Plumbing Enemy Number One. He was one of the original P.L.U.N.G.E. agents, and with his black mask and secret identity, he's the spitting image of a superhero. Or a supervillain, depending on who you ask.

"I'll give you my bike for it," Nixon says. "No, wait…my computer. No, wait…a kidney."

"A kidney?"

"All right, two kidneys. That's all I have on me, but if you'll give me a day, I think I can get more."

"I'm not taking your vital organs, Nixon."

He shrugs.

"Suit yourself, but you're crazy if you don't cash in," he says, and the corners of his mouth curl up like a sinister mustache. "You know where you can get top dollar for stuff like this? The Burrito Festival."

He's right. If Nitro City is known for one thing besides exploding, it's the annual Burrito Festival. People come from all over, and not just for the plumber card trade-a-thon. They come for the parade, and the costume contest, and the crafts fair, and the recipe rodeo, but mostly they come for the burritos. There's every flavor you can possibly imagine, and a few you probably don't want to.

"Hello, losers."

The unmistakable smell of Heartthrob cologne and Salisbury steak tells me that Scott Turbin is standing right behind me. When I turn my head, he darts to the other side of my chair and grabs the cards off the table.

"Hey, those are mine!"

"Don't get your undies in a wad. I'm just looking."

Okay, I'm not blind, I can see he's just looking. But with Scott, there's a thin line between looking and taking, and I'd just as soon we didn't get anywhere near it.

Scott Turbin is one of the most popular kids in the eighth grade, mainly because he's got Hollywood teeth, skin like a dolphin, and hair that—as far as I know— has never moved. He looks like the "after" picture in a pimple-cream ad.

"Not bad, not bad," he says. "Tell you what, I'll give you five bucks for them."

"Just give them back to me, Scott."

"Hold on, we're still negotiating."

"Give them back."

I reach for the cards, but he yanks them away.

"Relax!" he shouts, causing every head in earshot

to turn our way. "You can have them back when I'm done."

Who is he kidding? He's never going to be done. Scott doesn't care about plumber cards, he just likes being a jerk. Unfortunately, I don't have a lot of options. If I try to take them, the cards could get ripped up in the struggle. But if I do nothing, then—

"Whoa! Are those plumber cards?"

A blond girl appears out of nowhere and, with the easy touch of a pickpocket, snatches the stack from Scott's fingers. Her blue eyes light up as she thumbs through them.

"You've got Amber Waves? No way, she's my favorite!"

I raise an eyebrow.

"You know about Amber Waves?"

"I know she's underrated," she says. "I mean, her career didn't last long, but she was one of the greats of the Golden Age."

My mouth falls wide open. That's exactly what I would've said.

Scott moves between us and flashes his perfect teeth.

"Hi, I'm—"

"Scott Turbin. I know," the girl says. "We're in the same homeroom. You sit with those guys in the very back, right?"

"You should come hang out with us," he tells her. "But bring a sweater. My group is so cool, we actually lower the temperature of the room."

"And the I.Q.," Nixon says.

The girl smiles.

Her name is April Danvers. I don't know much about her except she transferred to Gloomy Valley at the start of this semester, but I heard she's smart. And she knows her plumbers. I'll give her that much.

She glances at her watch.

"Oh, gotta get to class. I'll see you in homeroom," she says, turning to leave.

Scott clears his throat.

"Aren't you forgetting something?"

"Oh, my gosh!" April groans, sounding embarrassed. "Where's my head? If there's one thing I can't stand, it's a thief."

She looks at Scott and holds out the cards. But when he reaches for them, she makes a quick turn and stuffs them inside my shirt pocket. I'm stunned. Before I can say anything, she gives me a wink and strolls out of the cafeteria.

Wow. Five minutes ago, I barely knew April Danvers existed. Now I think she's my favorite person on the planet.

I turn around and find Scott glaring at me. He looks like he just swallowed a lemon.

"Okay, you got your stupid cards back. Happy now, sewer boy?"

As a matter of fact, I am happy. Well, except about being called sewer boy. Of all the nicknames in the world, why did I have to get stuck with that one?

Chapter 10

Friday, 4:27 p.m.

I was eight years old the first time I crossed into the Underworld. Six hours later, I was in the back of a police car wrapped in a blanket and being told everything was going to be all right. The officer who found me—I think his name was Jones? Johnson? It was something like that. Anyway, they gave him a commendation. I remember seeing his picture in the paper and thinking it was strange he was getting an award for saving the "little lost sewer boy." I mean, he did find me, and he seemed like a nice enough guy, but here's the thing...

I wasn't lost.

That was five years ago. You'd think people would have forgotten, but every now and then, someone still calls me "sewer boy." As nicknames go, it's pretty much the worst. Unfortunately, in my case—it fits.

I know a dozen different ways to get into the sewer. The manholes are supposed to be sealed, but they can't get them all. This one's behind an old gas station, completely covered in litter and weeds. It's not my favorite entrance, but it's out of the way and, more important, out of sight. I can't explain it, but all day long I've had the strangest feeling people are watching me. Like at school, I could've sworn I caught three different kids staring at me in the hall. It wasn't a straight-on stare, it was the kind you give people with bad haircuts, or toilet paper stuck to their shoe. I don't know, maybe they weren't looking at me at all. It was probably my imagination.

Either that or I'm paranoid. Max says it happens to everybody eventually. Everybody in our business, anyway. It's a side effect of always having to look over your shoulder.

Which reminds me…

I look back over my shoulder. There's no one around, so I slide back a rotting plywood sign, then disappear into the earth like a weasel into its burrow.

The first thing you notice about the Underworld is that it's dark. Not pitch dark—it's more like you're wearing three pairs of sunglasses at the same time. The good news is, after a minute or so, your eyes start to adjust.

The bad news is, you're probably not going to like what you see.

I walk down the tunnel, but don't get far. Because I'm not alone. Straight ahead, there are two bloodred eyes glowing in the shadows. I give whatever's looking my way a good, hard stare. It doesn't blink. Carefully, I reach into my backpack and pull out a flashlight, then hit it in the eyeballs with the high beam.

Great, a sewer rat. I'll be honest, not my favorite vermin. They're mean as badgers, filthy as pigs, and smell like a skunk in an elephant's butt. And as for looks? Well, let's just say when rats throw parties, nobody asks them to dance.

This one's about the size of a pit bull—a pit bull that spends a lot of time at the gym. I take a step forward and, thankfully, he moves back. When he turns and runs down the tunnel, I scrunch up my shoulders until I've squeezed out the last of the creepiness. Jeez, those things give me the willies. Still, I'd be lying if I said I wasn't relieved—I mean, there are worse things down here than rats. A lot worse. I remember this one time, I was—

Krrrack.

I hear something...something close. Suddenly, I feel a cold hand on my shoulder. The fingers are long and bony, but the grip is strong. I jerk my head around and see two black eyes and a grim, skeletal face looking back at me.

It's the Moleman.

Chapter 11

Friday, 5:12 p.m.

"Oh, hey, Moleman."

"Hello, Sullivan. Why so jumpy today?"

"No reason," I tell him. "I just didn't know it was you."

"Oh? Were you expecting someone else?"

I shake my head. "No."

"Are you sure?"

His voice isn't threatening, but I'd be lying if I said it wasn't menacing.

"Yes, I'm sure. No one knows I come to see you, Moleman. Do you really think I'd blab about that?"

He doesn't answer right away. He just stares at me with those sinister black eyes. But after a few seconds, his face breaks into something that looks a lot like a grin. Or a grimace. To be honest, it's pretty hard to tell.

"Of course you wouldn't," he says. "Come along, Sullivan."

Without another word, he waves a long, thin hand in the air and walks down the path. I fall in behind him.

We move through the tunnel until we reach a patch of concrete that looks exactly like every other patch of concrete in the sewer, but somehow the Moleman knows just where to find it. He presses his hands against the wall, and like magic, a passage creaks open.

Did I mention the Moleman is a supervillain? Well, a retired supervillain, but he used to be a pretty big-name criminal. In fact, back in the Golden Age, he came very close to taking over the entire sewer. I don't think he's ever gotten over the fact that it was a bunch of plumbers who stopped him. Still, as evil geniuses go, he's really not a bad guy.

We step through the opening, head down a dark concrete alley, and finally stop in front of a heavy steel door.

Beside it is an electronic keypad. The Moleman raises a finger.

"Close your eyes, Sullivan."

It feels silly, but I do it. I hear a few beeps, then a whooshing noise, and the heavy door slides open.

There it is—the Moleman's underground lair.

At first glance, it's a pretty scary-looking place. But then he claps twice, which is how you turn on the lights, and it brightens right up. I don't have a lot to compare it to, but my guess is it looks pretty much like any other scientist's lair. There's a lab table, a computer, some torture devices, a coffee maker—the usual stuff. On the wall are two posters: a cat asking "Is It Friday Yet?" and a big yellow smiley face with a scar and an eye patch.

The Moleman takes off his black hat and raincoat, and the transformation is amazing. Now, instead of a terrifying monster who roams the sewers, I'm looking at a tall, thin man with long, spindly arms and legs. His hair is dark with streaks of white running down the sides, and he has skinny black eyebrows that curl up on the ends. Standing here in his brown slacks, gray sweater, and tie, he doesn't look like a supervillain at all. He looks like an accountant.

An evil accountant, but still.

"So have you got anything for me today?" I ask.

He strokes his long chin.

"Hmmmm...I've been working on a couple of things, but nothing that's going to set the world on fire," he says. "Did you want to set the world on fire?"

I shake my head, and he lets out a sad sigh. I'm pretty sure the Moleman is hoping I have an abominable side that just hasn't come out yet.

"Oh, well, I'm sure we can find something you can use," he tells me. "Let's see—secret inventions, secret inventions...where did I put those? Ah! Over here."

He leads me to a cardboard box sitting on a rickety old table in the back corner. It's full of wicked-looking gadgets in various stages of development. I go after them like a kid in a madman's candy store.

"Cool!"

"Eh," says the Moleman, wrinkling up his nose. "I used to turn out better junk in my sleep. Of course, I had a whole evil team back then. You know what they say, you can't spell 'menace' without 'men.'"

Sometimes I think the Moleman misses the old days. He gave up trying to take over Nitro City a long time ago, but he still likes to tinker around in the lab.

Apparently, twisted genius isn't something you can just turn off like a faucet.

As for me, I'm sort of his unpaid test dummy, but only if I see something I like.

"What's this one?" I ask.

I hold up a plastic bag with five black capsules.

"Oh, that's Death-Lax," the Moleman says. "Take just one pill and it's like eating thirty bowls of industrial-strength bran flakes. Take just one pill and you can shut down a bathroom for hours."

"What if I take two pills?"

"They evacuate your block and bury your toilet under a salt dome in the desert," he says.

I look through the rest of the box, hoping there's something better than super-laxatives. But it's the same old stuff I've seen before: the Death-Light, the Death-Wrench, the Death-Comb 3000, which are really just exploding versions of the things they look like.

"Why do you name all your inventions Death-something?" I ask.

"Brand management," the Moleman says. "You should always be reinforcing your brand, Sullivan. It's the first thing they teach you in business school."

"You went to business school?"

"Of course. How do you think I got so evil?"

I grab a couple of gadgets out of the box, but it's mostly just to be polite. I don't think there's anything here I can use. I'm about to leave when I notice something lying on top of the wastebasket.

I pick it up. It's a round silver casing with a thick metal coil inside.

"What's this do?"

"Nothing. It's just a retractable drain snake," the Moleman says. "I put a little claw on the end and added a more powerful motor—I thought it might turn into something diabolical. But just look at it. I mean, what's terrifying about that?"

"Can I have it?" I say.

He gives me the look—the one that tells me he's filled with disappointment. The Moleman has never understood my attraction to nondestructive objects. But he nods, and I stick it in my backpack.

We walk down the passage that leads back to the main tunnel. When we reach the end, I bring up the real reason I came here today.

"Hey, Moleman, have you noticed anything weird happening in the sewer lately?"

"Weird?"

"Stuff that would affect the plumbing," I say.

He'll never admit it, but very little happens in the Underworld that the Moleman doesn't know something about. He's got eyes everywhere. I tell him about the mutants, and the pipes breaking, and what Leonard said about the school's drains slowing down. I mean, individually, they're no big deal, but put them together...

"Well, I only know what I read in the papers," he says. "I'm just an old retired scientist, Sullivan. I mind my own business. But if you're asking for my opinion, I'd say that the Ironwater Corporation is a very, very efficient organization. If something's going on with the plumbing, you can be sure they know all about it. Remember, they're the company that built the Nitrodome."

"I guess you're right," I say. "So there's nothing to worry about?"

The Moleman gives me an odd look, and one of his eyebrows rises into a disturbing arch.

"Oh, I didn't say that, Sullivan," he tells me. "I didn't say that at all."

And he closes the door.

Chapter 12

Friday, 6:36 p.m.

What did he mean by that? It's going to bug me all day.
Just once, I wish I could get an answer from the Moleman that didn't sound like it came out of a fortune
cookie. It must be a supervillain thing.

I walk down the tunnel until I can't go any farther.
There's a massive wall blocking my path. I knew it was
here, that's why I came this way...just to look at it. It's
one of the wonders of the world.

The Nitrodome.

Even now, it seems impossible—an enormous

concrete-and-steel shell that covers a quarter of the Underworld. It has no doors, no hatches, no way in and no way out, and for the past fifteen years, it's been Nitro City's greatest mystery. I touch it with my hand, trying to imagine what's inside. I mean, I know it's supposed to be some kind of giant, high-tech mutant filter, but no one really knows how it works. No one but Ironwater, and they aren't talking.

I hate it, of course. I hate every terrible, beautiful inch of it. Every plumber does. Still, something keeps pulling me here. It's been pulling me here since I was eight years old.

I turn around and head back the way I came.

The manhole cover sticks for a second, but then it pops open. That's a relief. Getting trapped underground is kind of my biggest fear. I crawl out of the hole, stomp through the weeds, and walk toward the deserted gas station.

"Hello, young fella."

At least it *used* to be deserted.

The man is tall and thin, with a blue work shirt and aviator sunglasses. His head is shaved, and he's leaning up against the side of the building like he's been waiting for me. But since I didn't tell anyone I was coming here, how did he know where I'd be?

The way I see it, there are only two possibilities:

1. I was right about being watched; or
2. The bald guy is me from the future.

Man, I hope it's not number two.

"Who are you?" I ask.

"You can call me Cowboy," the man says.

Cowboy? That doesn't tell me much. Still, standing here close like this, I can see the embroidered initials on the pocket of his shirt: I.C.K.

Ironwater Control Keepers.

Great. He's an Ick.

"What do you want?"

"Relax, partner. I just want to talk to you."

"Talk about what?"

A creepy grin crosses his face.

"Don't you know?"

The truth is, between Leonard, Max, and the Moleman, I can think of about a dozen reasons Ironwater would want to talk to me. I just don't know which one Cowboy has in mind.

"No idea," I tell him.

He wipes a hand across his baby-smooth scalp and takes a step toward me.

"So you're saying you haven't done anything?"

"That's right."

"And you don't know anything?"

"I don't."

"And you're not the Toilet King?"

"I'm...what?"

I can't believe it. They've got the wrong guy. Wow... who would've thought I might actually be innocent? The Toilet King? I mean, I've been called a lot of things in my time, but never anything that stupid.

"No, I am definitely not the Toilet King," I tell him.

Cowboy sighs and puts a cell phone to his ear.

"All right, I've got him. You can come on down now."

A shiny black SUV appears in the distance and slowly makes its way down the street. It's an Ick car. You can tell because it looks like something they rent out for funerals. I get a sick feeling in the pit of my stomach.

"Look, you've got the wrong guy. I can prove who I am."

I unzip my backpack and reach inside.

"Kid, I don't need to see your ID."

That's good. Because I don't have one. What I do have is a big flowery can that says "Air Freshener," and I point it at his face.

"What are you going to do with that?" he says. "Deodorize me?"

I don't answer. I just press the button. A second later, Cowboy gets a face full of Death-Stink 3000, one of the Moleman's more nauseating creations. He winces in skunk-scented agony, and while he's still in mid-gag, I shove past him and make a break for the open field.

I've barely cleared the curb when I hear the SUV's engine roar, and I glance back over my shoulder. It's coming up fast.

This might've been a mistake.

I should swerve. Isn't that what you're supposed to do? Run in little zigzags to keep the pursuer off-balance? Or maybe that only works for animals. I don't know, I've never tried to outrun a car before! And from the way it's gaining on me, I don't think it's something I'm going to be good at.

I make a hard cut to the left and race into the tall weeds. The metal beast mows them down like a tractor. What was I thinking, trying to lose an SUV in a field? Fields are their natural habitat!

I've got one chance, but it's a longshot. At the far end of the property, there's a large culvert running underneath a road. If I can get there first, I can crawl through—it's the one place the SUV can't follow me. My neighborhood is on the other side. I'll be home free.

But it's at least a hundred yards away, and my lungs already feel like they're going to burst. I head toward the culvert. The Icks match my speed.

Fifty yards to go…then forty…then thirty. The opening is dead ahead. I sprint for it, sucking air like a wheezy vacuum cleaner, and that's when I feel something thick and hard, and…owwwwww!

Painful.

It's a rock. Maybe the only rock in the entire field, and I somehow managed to trip over it.

My body slams against the ground. The SUV comes to a stop a few feet away. Instantly, the doors fly open like escape hatches. Three Icks jump out.

"Oh, my gosh, I could barely breathe in there!" says the driver, a big-bellied, bushy-haired goon. "I thought I was going to be sick."

"Shut up!" Cowboy tells him, then turns to look at me. "I guess you think your little spray-can stunt was pretty clever. Well, we'll see who's laughing when this is over."

The three of them come at me. I scoot away, but it's too late to run. And then I hear something. It's a faint, distant hum, like a swarm of angry bees. And it's getting louder.

Out of nowhere, a sleek, shimmering motorcycle speeds across the field, sliding to a stop between me and the Icks. The rider looks like a faceless shadow— black helmet, black jacket, black boots. Before I can say a word, the bike seat is empty, and the bushy-haired Ick is laid out on the ground—along with two of his teeth.

Cowboy points at the rider. "Hey! You better get back on that bike and just—"

He doesn't finish his sentence. He can't, because there's a black boot in his mouth. As gracefully as an acrobat, the rider makes a low spin move, sweeping Cowboy's legs out from under him. He drops like the temperature in January.

"Look out!" I yell.

But not in time. The third Ick, a large, stocky man with a beard, grabs the rider from behind. It's a vicious, crushing bear hug—but it doesn't last. An elbow to the rib cage doubles the big guy over. A palm-strike to the nose puts him down.

I'm stunned. All three of my attackers are out of commission, and the whole thing only took thirty seconds. I stare at the rider, trying to get a glimpse of my mysterious hero, but all I see is my own reflection in the helmet's face shield.

Then, as suddenly as it arrived, the sleek black bike streaks away.

I watch it for a second—and I mean literally one second—because I'm not sticking around. The Icks are already starting to stir.

So before they can get to their feet, I turn around, race to the culvert, and slip through the pipe. And I don't stop running until I'm upstairs in Big Joe's house.

Chapter 13

Saturday, 10:24 a.m.

"Hi, honey!" my mom's singalong voice rings out from the speaker on my computer.

There they are, my family, huddled together in matching T-shirts with my picture on the front. They've broken out the big smiles, the ones most people save for Christmas card photos.

"Hi!" I say, trying to imitate their enthusiasm.

"We misssssssssssssss yooooooooooooooooou!" they harmonize.

I miss them, too—my mom, my dad, even my little

sister, Emmy. When they left for Fiji, we promised we'd talk face-to-face every single day. But you know how it is, there's a sixteen-hour time difference, and it's tough to match up schedules. But we do it as often as we can.

"So, how's everybody doing?" I ask.

My mom's eyes light up like Roman candles.

"We're at code red," she squeals. "The omelet craze has just hit the Fiji Islands!"

Omelets are a big deal to my mom. She's the regional sales director for Spatula World, the third-largest spatula manufacturer in the country. She loves her job, and she's good at it. With blond hair and industrial-strength dimples, she's like a drop of sunshine that fell to Earth and immediately started selling spatulas.

"Remember two years ago when Montreal flipped out over pancakes?" she says. "We couldn't keep spatulas on the shelves. Well, I talked to the head office yesterday, and they're saying omelets could be bigger— bigger than Montreal! Can you imagine? It's like a dream! But I don't want to talk about work, I want to talk about you."

"Me?"

"We are so proud of you," Mom says.

"We sure are, son," Dad echoes.

"My big brother is the best!" says Emmy, sitting between them like an adorable blond Kewpie doll.

"Aw, come on, I haven't done anything," I say.

"Haven't done anything?"

Clearly, my mom is stunned by my humility. She starts listing some of my more noteworthy accomplishments.

"Your teacher says you're doing very well in English…"

Which is true.

"And your grades are up in algebra…"

They had nowhere to go but up.

"And you might make the debate team!"

This is news to me, as I don't plan on going out for the debate team. But my mom really likes debate, and arguing with her would only prove how great I'd be at it.

"And, oh, those e-mails I've gotten from your principal! He is very impressed with you, young man!"

Good ol' Leonard. It's amazing how much goodwill you can buy with toilet repair.

On the screen, my family beams at me like I'm a new baby or a really nice car. The unconditional love is overwhelming—and trust me, I can use all I can get. I want to tell them everything—about the Moleman,

Max, the Icks, the motorcycle rider—but I can't. Not now.

For maybe the first time in my life, they're actually proud of me.

I hear a phone ringing and see my mom pick up...a spatula? She points to it and smiles.

"It's called a chat-ula," she tells me. "It's a spatula with a phone in the handle so you can talk while you cook. Can you believe it? They're going to be huge!"

She looks down at the spatula phone.

"Oh, it's work, I've got to take this," she says. "Fill your dad in on everything. I loooooooooove you!"

"Love you, too!" I say.

Dad's wide smile follows her as she leaves the room.

"Take your time, hon!" he calls out. "We'll finish up here with the superstar!"

I hear a door close, and see Dad's lean, likable face rotate back toward the screen. But it's no longer the smiling, happy, suntanned face of a proud Dr. Jekyll. It's the red, twisted face of an angry Mr. Hyde!

"What is wrong with you?" he whisper-screams at me.

His short brown hair is standing on end. His kind eyes are on fire.

"What do you mean?" I say.

Frantically, he reaches into his pocket and pulls out a sheet of paper. He waves it in front of the computer's camera, and I can see that it's a picture—a picture of me standing on a toilet and holding a plunger up like a royal scepter. Underneath it are these words: "The Toilet King."

Izzy!

"The Toilet King?" Dad moans. "My son is the Toilet King? You demolished someone's bathroom!"

Emmy shoves her face in front of the camera.

"You're an embarrassment to the family!" she seethes, poking my screen image with her finger. "You think it's easy being the sister of a world-famous doofus?"

Emmy is in kindergarten, but she bullies at a ninth-grade level. We're very proud.

Dad pulls her back.

"How did you get that?" I ask.

"It's on the web," he says, his voice as exasperated as I've ever heard it. "The *world wide* web!"

"I'm sorry! But I can—"

"Have you got any idea how hard it's been to keep

this from your mother?" he says. "If she figures out how to pull up the internet on that spatula, you're sunk, buddy!"

"I can explain!"

"Really? Well it better be a king-sized explanation," he says, clutching Izzy's photo in his kung fu grip. "Look, son, things like this can't keep happening. Remember what your mother said after your last suspension?"

Remember? How could I forget? She said if I got into any more trouble—ever—I'd be going to military school. And not just any military school—Basher Academy: the Alcatraz of education.

"I know, believe me, I know," I tell him. "But just calm down. Your face is turning pur—"

Uh-oh. I almost said it—the forbidden word. See, ever since the disaster at the poetry contest, our family has avoided anything to do with "purple." It's not that we're against the color, it's just that it's still kind of a touchy subject with my dad.

"*Pur*-fect," I say, expertly covering my tracks. "Your face is turning *pur-fect*. That ocean air must be good for your skin."

Dad glares at me.

"Thank you," he growls. "And from now on, I'll be expecting *pur-fect* behavior from you."

"Oh, don't worry, you're going to get it," I say.

"Screw up again, and *you're* going to get it!" Emmy yells.

If my dad hadn't been there, I really believe she would've punched the screen.

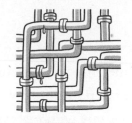

Chapter 14

Monday, 3:59 p.m.

"You knew I was the Toilet King the whole time? And you didn't tell me?"

"It was funny," Nixon says.

"But I was the only one who didn't know. It made me look like an idiot!"

"That was the funny part," he says.

The veins in my temples start to throb.

We're sitting in a red vinyl booth in our favorite hangout, Griddle Buns, which is the best hot dog and waffle place in Nitro City, and possibly the world.

Nixon is across the table from me. I'm thinking of bludgeoning him with the mustard dispenser. Instead, I ignore him and look up at the TV set in the corner. It's showing an older guy with big white teeth, a light-blue sweater, and a tie. He's walking by a peaceful-looking lake.

"Hi. I'm Herman Wiest, chairman of the Ironwater Corporation. You know, at Ironwater, we don't just believe in a good, clean sewer system. We believe in good, clean fun," he says. *"That's why we're proud to be the official sponsor of Nitro City's Fiftieth Anniversary Burrito Festival. There will be lots to eat, lots to do, and no-wait, state-of-the-art restrooms for your comfort and convenience. So come join us at the Burrito Festival. Like we always say: If you don't like it, you can stuff it…with your choice of over one hundred popular fillings!"*

"You know, it's coming up pretty fast," Nixon says, staring at the screen.

"So?"

"So we should get our tickets now," he says.

I cross my arms.

"Our tickets?" I say. "You think I'm going with you after you didn't tell me about that picture? What kind of a best friend are you?"

"The kind who can do *this*," he says.

He picks up the hot dog on his plate, rolls it inside a waffle, and stuffs the entire thing in his mouth longways. His cheeks blow up like two microwave popcorn bags.

It doesn't make up for everything, but it makes up for a lot.

"I'm still going to get you for this."

"Ahmmmm reeel scurrrrred," he chews.

I give him a menacing look, then pull out my phone and start pecking at the tiny keyboard. Nixon gags, gulps, and swallows.

"What are you doing?" he asks.

"I'm trying to find P.L.U.N.G.E."

"Did you check ancient history? Because I'm pretty sure that's the last place I saw them."

If Nixon has an off button, I haven't found it yet.

"Some of them are still around. I've seen stories on the news," I say.

"You mean those stories about them blowing up sewer pipes and shutting down bathrooms?" Nixon says.

He dangles a curly fry over his open mouth, then gobbles it down like a baby bird going after a worm.

"They don't do that kind of stuff because they're bad, they do it because they're standing up to Ironwater," I tell him, sounding a little more defensive than I thought I would. "Anyway, I want to know how to contact them just in case those Icks try to grab me again."

"Contact them? For what?" he asks.

"Protection."

"Protection?"

Okay, maybe "protection" isn't the right word. What I really need is a guardian angel, preferably one that rides a motorcycle and has ninja moves. I don't know if my mysterious rescuer is part of P.L.U.N.G.E., but who else would have the guts to take on Ironwater? Besides, when it comes to the hero business, P.L.U.N.G.E. is just about as good as it gets.

I punch in another search.

"Any luck?" Nixon asks.

"No. There's nothing about how to get in touch with them."

"Well, duh," he says. "They're outlaws. Did you really think they'd be listed in the phone book?"

To be totally honest, I didn't know. The truth is, except for Max and the Moleman, I've had surprisingly little contact with the outlaw world. That's why it's so weird that, of all people, the Icks would be coming after me. Especially over some stupid picture.

I try another search. Nothing.

"It's hopeless. I'm doomed."

"Probably," Nixon says, licking a disgusting yellow-brown mixture off his plate. "Or maybe you're just using the wrong internet."

Instinctively, my hand reaches for an onion ring to chuck at him. But he looks serious.

"What do you mean?"

"You should look on darknet. It's the internet for people who don't want you to know what they're up to."

Hmmm...I'd never heard of darknet. It sounded tempting and dangerous, like a birthday cake full of firecrackers.

"Great. How do I get on it?"

"*You* don't," he says. "The whole point of having a darknet is so that people like you can't use it. No, if you want to go to the dark side, you'll need someone who knows the territory. Someone who's corrupt, underhanded, devious..."

"That's you," I say.

"You flatter me. But in this case, they also have to have computer skills."

"So what'll I do?"

Nixon leans back against the red vinyl cushion. The indentation surrounds his head like a fiery halo.

"Give me a few days," he says. "I might know somebody."

Chapter 15

Thursday, 8:24 a.m.

You know that dream where you're at school and you suddenly realize you forgot to put on pants? That's my life now. As I move through the hall, I see kids staring and laughing. They call me "Your Highness" and "Your Majesty," and even though that's nicer than what they usually call me, it still stings.

The Toilet King is officially the funniest thing to hit Gloomy Valley since they ran Andy Niedermeyer's underwear up the flagpole. Of course, that was only funny because Andy was still in them.

Middle school is a cruel and terrible place.

I walk into homeroom. Mr. Gooseberry, as usual, is hidden behind his newspaper. In all the time I've been in this class, I don't think I've ever seen his face. Not that I need to—I mean, what's a homeroom teacher do, anyway? Take roll, and make sure the kids don't eat each other. By that standard, Mr. G is doing a pretty bang-up job.

I ignore the gawking heads and sneak down the third row.

"Mr. Gooseberry?" I say.

"Yes?" says the voice behind the newspaper.

"Can I change desks?"

"Is yours on fire?"

"No."

"Then no."

Mr. G. has one rule: unless something's bleeding, on fire, or giving out money, he doesn't want to know about it. Which is too bad because I've just reached my desk, and there's a toilet seat where my butt needs to be.

Scott Turbin and his friends are in the corner laughing so hard they can barely stay in their chairs.

"Mr. Gooseberry?"

"What now, Sully?"

I look around. Everyone is watching me.

"Never mind."

I lift the lid and sit down. It's humiliating but, if I'm being totally honest, surprisingly comfortable.

Scott moves to the desk next to mine. He's staring at me, and it's getting annoying. I guess I could ignore his goofy grinning face and just wait for the bell to ring, but it's probably best to get this over with.

"What do you want, Scott?"

"KA-POOOOOOOSH!" Scott says, making a loud flushing noise with his mouth. Then he laughs like a deranged hyena and wanders back to his corner.

I put my head on my desk.

"Do you want me to take that away?"

When I look up, April Danvers is standing beside me. She's wearing a pink shirt with little yellow flowers that match her hair.

"I can get that seat out of here. They'll stop laughing then," she says.

"No, it's fine," I say. "I mean, a king's got to have a throne, right? But thanks."

"All right, but if you change your mind, you know where I sit," she says.

I do know where she sits: front row, second chair from the left. It's a prime location for smart kids, and not just because of the excellent pencil-sharpener access. By being close to the teacher, front-row kids are completely separated from all the chaos in the back of the room. I could never be part of their world, but that doesn't mean I don't admire it from afar.

She turns to leave, then stops and looks back over her shoulder.

"Oh, and just so you know, I saw that picture everyone's talking about, and I really don't think it's that bad."

"It's not?"

She shakes her head.

"It's actually kind of cute. Have you ever thought about modeling?"

April smiles at me, and her blue eyes sparkle. Then she heads back to her power position at the front of the room. The second she's gone, I feel a little tingle run down my spine. Then another one. Then another one. When I look up, I see why. Huge, wet drops are falling from the ceiling above my desk. Hmmm...must be some kind of leak. Which means it has to be coming from—

Uh-oh.

Suddenly, the realization hits me and I start to dive out of the way. But I'm a second too late.

The acoustic-tile ceiling gives way and a gusher of toilet water pours down from the upstairs restroom. It drenches me, and most of the kids around me, and I don't need to be a front-row student to know this was no accident.

I leap out of my desk and run toward the door.

"I'm going to the restroom!" I yell.

"Whatever," Mr. G says, waving at me from behind his paper.

When I reach the upstairs boys' room, I find a half dozen students gathered in the hall, which makes checking the floor for wet footprints useless. Too many people have tracked through the scene.

I roll my eyes and open the restroom door. Leonard is already inside. So is Mr. Krumsky, our janitor, who growls at me as I slosh across the waterlogged tiles.

"Is it...?" Leonard asks me.

A Torpedo brand cigarette butt floats past my feet.

"Yeah. It's the Phantom."

When I get to the stall, I notice a peculiar scent—one that doesn't belong in a bathroom. I just wish I could remember where I've smelled it before.

As for the rest of the scene, it's pretty typical. The Phantom followed his standard routine, filling the bowl with paper, trash, and cigarette butts, then disabling the fill-float so the water would continue to run. But there is one thing that's different about this particular toilet.

It's missing its seat.

Chapter 16

Friday, 4:27 p.m.

After school, Nixon and I catch the subway and head over to the Black Hole, a scruffy-looking coffee shop where people wear sandals and stare at their laptop screens. Nixon calls it "Hackerland," probably because of all the hackers. It's our entrance to the shadowy world of the dark web.

We head toward the back of the building.

"These don't look like the kind of people who are going to want to help a couple of kids," I say.

"Just don't freak out," Nixon whispers. "Whatever happens, promise me you won't freak out."

"Why? What's going to happen?"

He doesn't answer. He doesn't need to.

I spy her sitting in a dimly lit booth in the back corner. Her eyes say she's dangerous, but her T-shirt says she's weird. Literally—she has on a gray T-shirt that says I'M WEIRD in big black letters. What kind of a person wears something like that?

I'll tell you what kind: Izzy Cisco.

"You!" I freak out.

"Are you going to sit down? Or did you just come in to smash up the restroom?" she says.

Izzy takes a sip out of a coffee mug the size of a cereal bowl. I stare at Nixon with my mouth wide open, but no words are coming out. What was he thinking? Izzy Cisco isn't the answer to my problems. Izzy Cisco is the reason for my problems!

Nixon plops down next to her.

"Now, before you explode, just remember you wanted me to find somebody who could get on the dark web, right? Well, that automatically ruled out anyone nice," he says, then glances at Izzy. "No offense."

"None taken, dork-bag," she tells him, her eyes never leaving the computer screen.

Reluctantly, I sit down in the booth.

"You really know about this stuff?" I ask. "About... the dark web?"

She gives me the look that's always on her face at school—the one that says she knows everything.

"Well...thanks, then."

"For what?" she says.

"For helping me. Not everybody would do this for their archnemesis."

"My what?"

"Your archnemesis," I tell her. "You know, your mortal enemy, your chief rival...the scourge of your existence?"

She stops typing. Her forehead wrinkles up like an unmade bed.

"Mortal enemy? I barely even know you."

Okay, now she's just talking crazy. Maybe we don't exchange death threats or scream insults across the cafeteria, but that doesn't mean there isn't something special between us. If anything, the fact that we never spend time together only proves how much we can't stand each other.

"Come on, you're always calling me sewer boy."

"That's because I can't remember your name," she says.

Her face is blank and serious, and I get a weird, squishy feeling in my stomach. Is it really possible Izzy Cisco doesn't think horrible thoughts about me day and night? No. No one would work this hard to convince me I wasn't hated unless they really, truly despised me. I make her skin crawl and she knows it.

"So what kind of trouble are you in, anyway?" she says.

I take a deep breath and tell her about the black SUV, and the man with the shaved head, and having to sit on a toilet seat in homeroom.

"Plus, my dad yelled at me all the way from Fiji, and I might have to go to military school."

Izzy's eyes widen, and then she lets out a huge laugh. It's annoying.

"Are you going to help me or not?" I ask her.

"All right, all right. Don't get your pantaloons in a wad, Your Majesty."

She stretches her fingers, then places them on the

keys—keys I'm hoping will open the forbidden doors of the dark web.

What happens next goes by in a blur. Izzy downloads some information, enters a strange-looking code, and covers up the camera on her computer to make sure we're not being watched. Then she mutters a magic spell, but I'm pretty sure that's just to freak me out.

And then we're in.

"That's it?" Nixon says. "I thought it'd be eviler."

I thought so, too. But it turns out the dark web looks a lot like the regular web. Which is pretty disappointing, considering it's the badlands of the internet.

"So what do you want me to search for?" Izzy asks.

I'm just about to tell her when Nixon blurts out—

"Bigbutt!"

"No!" I tell him. "We're not looking up Bigbutt."

"What's the matter? Scared we'll find out the truth?" he says.

I sigh. According to legend, Bigbutt is a large, smelly creature who roams the woods outside Nitro City, leaving gigantic butt-prints wherever he sits. Nixon is his biggest fan.

"Okay, but just for a minute," I mumble.

Izzy punches it in. A millisecond later, we see a blurry black-and-white photo of what looks like a guy in a bear suit sitting on two balloons. There's also a bunch of stuff about UFOs, and a clearly fake picture of the Lake Nitro Monster.

Nixon shakes his head. "Man, this is one weird town."

"All right, you've seen it," I say. "Now can we focus on why we're here?"

I turn to Izzy.

"Put in 'How to contact P.L.U.N.G.E.'"

"P.L.U.N.G.E.?" she says, looking like a bug just flew into her mouth. "Why would you want to contact them?"

I glare at her. Why wouldn't I want to contact them? P.L.U.N.G.E. is the most amazing assembly of plumbing talent ever put together. Izzy might think they're the bad guys, but to me they'll always be the superheroes of the sewer.

"Will you just do it?" I say.

She rolls her eyes, then types in P.L.U.N.G.E. A long row of hits appears on the screen. Most of them look like fan sites with stories about the old days. She clicks on one.

"That's P.L.U.N.G.E.?" she says. "It looks like a comic book convention."

The photo shows a large group of plumbers decked out in their full costumes. It's from the Golden Age, back when masks and capes were sort of the big thing.

"Who's the guy in the crash helmet?" Nixon asks.

I look at the picture.

"Tiny Dinkins."

"Tiny?" he says. "He's huge!"

He's right, Tiny Dinkins was an absolutely enormous human being. I don't know if he's still around, but I think I can definitely rule him out as the motorcycle rider. In fact, now that I look at them, most of these plumbers would be way too big. And they'd all be pretty old, too. It's hard to imagine any of them doing leg sweeps and roundhouse kicks in black leather pants.

"Where's the new stuff? The stuff about what P.L.U.N.G.E. is doing now?" I say.

Izzy clicks around, and we find a few articles on sewer-line backups and sabotaged equipment, the same stuff Pepper Hayes was talking about on the news. But there's nothing like what I was hoping for—secret messages, coded e-mails, and untraceable ways to get in touch with them.

"No, no, this isn't it, either."

"Well, it's not my fault," she says. "This is what's here. What were you expecting?"

"I was expecting some help!"

Suddenly, Nixon's face lights up, and he points to the screen.

"How about him? If you really want protection, he looks pretty terrifying."

"That's the Human Waste," I tell him. "He's a supervillain."

"So?"

"He's also dead," I say.

"Correction: He *was* dead," Nixon explains. "Look, it says right here he's come back from the grave...to seek revenge! Now show me that picture of Bigbutt again."

I shut my eyes and lean against the back of the booth. This whole thing has been a waste of time. It turns out the dark web is nothing but conspiracy theories and lies—and that's not going to save me from the

Icks. I might as well face it: I can't g
parents are in Fiji, and the Golden Ag
time ago.

I'm on my own.

Izzy shuts down the computer, and we walk outside. I check my phone.

Uh-oh. Two missed calls, and three texts from Big
Joe asking where I am.

I'm in trouble.

Chapter 17

Friday, 7:01 p.m.

The storm clouds are thick and gray like smoke over
the city. It's about to pour. I've felt it building for a
while now, and I get to Joe's house just as the rain
starts to ping around me like soft, wet BBs.

"Big Joe?" I say, but don't get an answer. Not that I
really want one. He's probably mad.

Besides, I can hear him messing around in the
garage. Figures. Old people always have a bunch of
stuff they have to do before it rains. They're like ants,
storing food and building up the walls of their mound.

I head upstairs to my room. When I open the door, I notice something is different, but it takes a second for it to set in.

They're gone.

All my posters, the faces of the people I admire most in the world, have vanished. Why? Because I was late? Because I missed his calls? It wasn't my fault—can I help it if coffee shops are loud? Oh, this is so typical of Big Joe—and just when I thought he'd changed, because he gave me those—

I rush to my desk and slide back the top right drawer—nothing. The plumber cards are gone, too.

Now I see what's going on—this isn't about the phone calls. It's just Joe's way of getting rid of anything that makes me happy. I keep forgetting my living here is supposed to be a punishment.

I can't exactly describe what I'm feeling inside. It's not rage—a volcano doesn't feel rage when it bursts open and spews lava and rock into the atmosphere. It's more like relief, letting go of a pressure that's been bubbling under the surface for way, way too long.

My feet fly down the stairs and I meet Joe at the door just as he's coming back into the house.

"Where are they?"

It's not a question, it's an accusation. I see surprise in his eyes, but then they go cold and narrow, like he's preparing for war.

"You need to calm down," he says.

"What gives you the right?"

It's the wrong thing to say. I know it even as the words are coming out of my mouth. There are a thousand ways to phrase that question, but the way I chose only leads to one answer.

"It's my house," he says.

His face is hard as stone, but he's right. It is his house—and I don't belong in it.

There's a crack of thunder, and I run out the front door, my sneakers splashing as I put space between me and my prison.

"Boy!" I hear him calling.

His voice gets lost in the pounding raindrops, and by the time I reach the corner, I can't hear it at all. The water feels like ice on my skin, and I'm glad. I want to feel numb. I want it to seep into my mind where I don't have to think about Joe, or my parents, or Leonard, or monsters, or black SUVs.

I don't know how long I've been out here. Long enough to be soaked through to my bones. Most of the shops on the street are closed, which is fine with me. I don't have my wallet, or my phone, so all I'd be after is a dry place to stand. And there are plenty of those around. I could go to Nixon's, or Max's, but I don't want to—I want to go home.

Only I don't know where that is anymore.

A pair of headlights turn onto the street. They move up slow and easy behind me, and when I swivel around for a look, I'm blinded by the bright beams shining in my eyes. As it rolls beside me, I recognize the faded baby-blue paint job and the dented bumper. The passenger door on the old Ford pickup swings open.

"You look like you could use a ride," Big Joe says.

"I'm fine," I tell him.

He nods.

"I know. Still, it beats walking in the rain."

I stop and look at him. The dome light in the truck gives me a good view of his face, but it doesn't tell me

111

a thing. Is he worried? Is he mad? Is he just getting me out of the weather, the same as he'd do for a stray dog?

I don't know. He just looks like Big Joe. And to me, that's a mystery. A chill climbs up my spine, and then, like the black cloud above me, I burst.

"Why did you want me to live with you, Big Joe? Because I'll tell you right now it's not going to work. It can't. I screw up everything. I screwed up so bad my parents moved halfway around the world without me. I'm always in trouble. I get kicked out of schools. And even when I try to help, I end up wrecking a bathroom or making everybody mad at me. I'm a screwup, Joe. And nobody wants to live with a screwup."

The words rush out fast and hard, and then I'm empty. I stand there, listening to the windshield wipers squeak back and forth across the glass. The rain is stopping.

"I'm hungry," Big Joe says. "You hungry? I feel like a chili burger. I haven't had one of those in a long, long time."

"Chili burger?" I say.

"Yeah. My treat."

We look at each other. He waits, and I wait. And then I climb inside and close the door.

Chapter 18

Friday, 8:57 p.m.

"Where are we going?" I ask.

I've got a shop blanket around me, the kind you put down to keep your tools from scratching somebody's floor. I found it behind the seat cushion, and it smells like hundred-year-old feet, but it's warm.

"I know a place," Joe says. "It's not fancy, but they've got the best chili burger I've ever tasted."

"You go there a lot?"

"I haven't been in years," he says.

We drive until we're out of our neighborhood, out

of the south side, and finally out of anything that resembles the civilized world. Instead, we're surrounded by shabby old buildings and rows of run-down businesses.

"You sure this is the right way?" I ask.

We pull into a dusty gravel parking lot and stop in front of a small stucco building that, a couple of decades ago, might have been white. Now it's sort of a dingy color, like an old sock you let the family dog chew on. The only bright thing about it is the roof, which holds a big, buzzing neon sign.

THE GOLDEN POO, it says.

I don't think it's supposed to say that. I think it's supposed to say THE GOLDEN SPOON but some of the letters are burned out. At least I hope so.

There's a misty rain falling. Joe pulls up near the entrance to let me out.

"You go on in while I park the truck," he says. "Ask the guy at the door what the pie is today."

I give him a strange look.

"They're famous for their pie," he says.

I nod and walk up to the door. There's a big guy standing out front. I mean really big—like he's holding up one of the walls.

"Where do you think you're going?" he asks me.

"Just inside," I say.

He cocks an eyebrow and crosses his arms.

"Oh, yeah? Why?"

All of a sudden, I feel nervous. Is it possible this place has changed since the last time Joe was here? Because it doesn't seem very family friendly.

"I…I heard you have great pie," I tell him. "What's the pie today?"

The man looks confused.

"You're here for pie?"

I nod.

"You sure?"

I nod again.

"Okay." He shrugs. "Go on in."

I walk around him—which is no short trip—and pass through a heavy black door. When I open it, I hear a ringing sound and look up. At the top, there's a tiny gold bell with a handwritten note next to it.

"Relax," the note says. "It's just a little tinkle."

That's weird. I've seen stuff like that before but always on bathroom doors, never one leading into a restaurant. I start to laugh, then wonder if I should call the health department.

Against my better judgment, I go inside.

The place isn't at all what I expected. I expected something dirty, with grease-stained walls and scary, dangerous-looking customers. This is much worse. I wouldn't call it a rat hole, exactly—rats have better taste. To be honest, it's tough to call it anything because it's so dark. The air is filled with smoke and cholesterol, and I'm trying not to breathe, but it's a hard habit to break. Even now, I can feel my lungs being coated in ancient French-fry oil.

Using the light of an electric beer sign, I manage to move across the sticky concrete floor until I come to an old pool table. There are no balls or cues, so I don't think anybody plays on it anymore. They probably just use it for other stuff, like holding stabbing victims until the ambulance arrives.

"You got some business here?" a big, grumpy-sounding man in a paper hat asks me.

He's standing behind a gritty chrome counter with a long row of barstools in front of it. When he talks, the room goes dead quiet.

I gulp.

"I'm here for pie," I say.

He stares at me.

"Pie? You?"

"I've heard good things," I tell him.

The man is enormous. Two thick arms bulge out of a white T-shirt that's covered by the special of the day—assuming the special of the day is filth. His sweaty face is round and pink, like a canned ham with ears, and it's something else...

It's familiar.

"You're...you're Tank Huberman," I wheeze.

Tank Huberman is the closest thing there is to plumbing royalty, and in a fairer world, his face would be on every toilet in America. Until earlier today, it held a large and treasured place on my bedroom wall.

"I know who I am, kid," he says. "The question is, who are you?"

Tank's beady eyes get beadier. He leans out over the counter, and when I look up at him, I forget how to make words.

"Sullivan Stringfellow," I finally squeak.

A huge laugh breaks out in the room. Only the Tank isn't laughing.

"Well...Sullivan Stringfellow," he growls. "Who sent you?"

"What?"

Now his eyes are peeling me like a potato.

"Who sent you here? Who told you about pie?"

I hear the heavy door open, the tiny, tinkling bell, and the sound of Big Joe's voice shouting, "I did."

There's a gasp from the crowd, and Tank Huberman's face goes completely pale. When I turn around, I see a man standing in the doorway wearing a black mask, and silver coveralls decorated with a pair of crossed white toilet plungers that form an unmistakable X. In a flash, the long absences and mysterious behavior that have puzzled me my whole life finally make sense.

Big Joe Feeney—my grandfather—is the Midnight Flush!

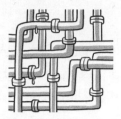

Chapter 19

Friday, 9:42 p.m.

You could hear a pin drop...on a pillow...in another state. That's how quiet it is in here.

And then it isn't.

Suddenly, the Golden Poo explodes. It's an act of spontaneous jubilation. The whole place is cheering like Big Joe just won the Super Bowl and a major war on the same day. They rush at him, slapping him on the back and shaking his hand, and if he were a thinner man, I'm pretty sure they'd lift him onto their shoulders and carry him around the room.

I can't believe it. Big Joe—the Midnight Flush.

The crowd parts and Joe makes his way to the counter, but he isn't looking at me. His eyes are locked onto the stunned man in the paper hat on the other side of the barstool. Tank Huberman doesn't say a word. He just blinks a couple of times like he's trying to wake up from a dream. Then, without warning, he springs forward and wraps Joe in a bear hug that, medically speaking, squish-ilates his internal organs.

"I knew you'd be back, Flush," Tank says. "I knew it. Now take off that stupid mask and let us have a look at you."

Joe grins and pulls off the mask that covers most of his head. The thick mop of gray hair comes popping out, and just like that, he's Big Joe again. But not the same Big Joe I knew a few minutes ago. That Joe is gone.

He slides onto a wobbly red stool and looks more comfortable than I have ever seen him.

"The old place hasn't changed a bit, Tank," he says. "Too bad. I thought you might've at least cleaned it."

Tank shakes his head.

"I like it this way. Reminds me of the pit."

When he says the pit, he means the sewer. A lot

of the old-time plumbers call it that. I glance around the room and see a bunch of gray heads nodding, like they're reliving fond memories of the worst place in the universe.

It makes zero sense, and I wish I could say I don't get it. But I do.

Big Joe looks at the crowd around him, and even though he's the most private person I know, he doesn't seem unhappy about the attention. His eyes freeze when they land on me, and he motions for me to join him.

"Listen, everybody, this is my grandson, Sully," he says, putting a hand on my shoulder.

The crowd roars like they're welcoming the heir to the throne.

"And, Sully, this worthless collection of outcasts, good-for-nuthins, rowdies, and sewer soldiers," he continues, "is P.I.E."

Pie?

"Plumbers In Exile," he proclaims, like the name is supposed to be famous. "The last, best hope for Nitro City."

I blink my eyes. Was he serious? These were Nitro City's ancient plumbing heroes? The feared knights of the sewer? I've got to admit, they aren't exactly what I'd imagined. A scrawny man missing his two front teeth rushes up to shake my hand.

"This is Ted Bentley," Big Joe tells me. "But you probably remember him as the Clogbuster."

The Clogbuster? Him? I couldn't believe it. But if Big Joe could be the Midnight Flush, I guess anything is possible.

He leads me through the room, introducing me to Molly "Under Woman" Cannon, Pete "Drainstorm" Contreras, Lady Leak, Emperor Commodius, and a dozen other titans of the pipe.

"Nice to meet you all," I say.

The crowd responds with another round of hooting and applause, and then it stops. Which is good, because some of them look like they need to sit down.

"So," Tank says. "What brings you back here?"

Joe's eyebrows curve downward until they look like a pair of hairy bat wings. He gives Tank a serious stare.

"You know why I'm back."

Tank nods slowly. He looks at the counter and runs a dirty dishrag across it.

"Maybe it won't be that bad," he says.

"It will," Joe tells him. "Are you ready?"

I notice Tank is intentionally avoiding Joe's eyes. What I don't know is why.

"Well, you see, the thing is, Joe, we're kind of..."

"Old," a gravelly voice in the corner says.

I whirl around and see what appears to be a small mountain sitting at the end of the counter. The man's butt cheeks melt over the sides of the stool like hot butter on a pancake.

I'd know that butt anywhere. It's Tiny Dinkins!

"That you, Melvin?" Big Joe says calmly, as if he speaks to legends every day. "My eyes don't work so good anymore."

"If you can't see something the size of me, you've gone stone blind," Tiny says.

His stool makes a slow, creaky swivel, and I can see a smile pushing up his pudgy jowls.

Wow. Tiny Dinkins.

Melvin "Tiny" Dinkins is a giant, and I don't just mean in the plumbing world. The man is as round as he is tall. Sitting there, he looks like a parade balloon that floated in the front door and decided to stay for dinner.

I peek at Big Joe. The grin on his face could light the room all by itself.

"What do you mean, old? You look terrific," Joe says. "You look like a million bucks."

"Jeez, your eyes really have gone bad, haven't they?" Tank says. "He looks old, Flush—old and tired. Just like me. Just like a lot of us. Look, I don't want you to get the idea we're not glad to see you, but the truth is…well, we feel like we've done enough for this town."

"And what's it gotten us?" Tiny says. "If you haven't heard, we're the bad guys. Why should we stick our necks out for people who want to lock us up?"

Big Joe's grin disappears. He glares at Tiny, then at Tank, and I see the muscles in his neck tighten. There's not a sound in the room. His eyes move from face to face as if he's seeing his friends—his *old* friends—for the first time.

"You want to know why?" he says, repeating Tiny's question. "You want to know why?" he says again, but louder this time, and he rises to his feet. "I'll tell you why. Tank…play B-5!"

A groan rolls out of the crowd.

"Joe, I don't think anybody wants to—"

"B-5!" he yells. "I think we could all use a little reminder."

Tank shrugs and walks over to an old-timey jukebox

that looks like it ought to be in a museum—a museum of garbage. He drops a couple of coins in the slot and pushes what I assume is the B-5 button. There's a pause, and a crackling noise from the speaker, and then an old song by a band called Men at Work starts playing. It's a cheerful tune about people who live in a "land down under," and as it plays, Big Joe spreads out his arms like he's trying to hug the air.

"Why do we stick our neck out?" he shouts. "Because we're plumbers—and we've been to the land down under!"

Joe taps his foot and nods his head to the music. I don't think he realizes the song is actually talking about Australia, and I'm not going to be the one to tell him. See, around here, the "land down under" means the sewer, and it has a special place in the heart of every plumber. As the final note plays, cheering and wild applause break out all over the Poo.

"Look, I know I've been gone a long time, and I'm sorry. It couldn't be helped," he tells the crowd. "And maybe I'm old, and maybe I'm not what I used to be, but you can flush all that. Because in my heart, I'm still a plumber. And I've still got a job to do."

There's another round of applause, but little by

little, it dies down until there's nothing left but silence. Before long, the smiles fade, too.

"They've pushed us out, Joe," Tank says quietly. "Ironwater won."

Big Joe gives him a long, sad stare, then closes his eyes.

"We'll see," he says. "We'll see."

Chapter 20

Saturday, 8:38 a.m.

It might've been a dream. What do I mean, "might?" Of course it was a dream! Big Joe? Tank Huberman? The Golden Poo? It's crazy.

Still, I've got the strangest feeling in the pit of my stomach, kind of happy and sick at the same time. My eyes pop wide open—because suddenly I know exactly what that feeling is.

It's a chili burger. The best I've ever tasted.

My whole life changed last night. Everything. And

the scariest part is, it turns out the cranky old man I'm sharing a house with really is a total stranger.

A totally awesome stranger, but still.

When I walk downstairs, Joe is dressed and waiting for me.

"So…" he says.

"So," I reply.

We both look at the floor.

"I guess you've got some questions," he mumbles.

I do. I have lots of questions. I have so many questions I can't hold them all in my brain, and when I open my mouth, they spill out in one all-encompassing super-question that goes something like this:

"So…the Midnight Flush?"

Joe sighs and runs a hand through his hair.

"Sit down, boy," he says.

I do.

"I never wanted to be the Flush. All I ever wanted to be was a decent husband to your grandmother, a good father to Teeny, and a real grampa for you and your sister," he says. "But it didn't work out that way."

"Because?"

"Plumbing," he says. "Every time I tried to let it go, somebody would turn on the spigot, I'd get caught in the current, and before I knew it, I'd be right back in the sewer."

"Just like me!"

"Yes, boy," he says. "Just like you."

Big Joe tells me about being a plumber in the Golden Age, a time when monsters were streaming through pipes like tap water. P.L.U.N.G.E. battled them around the clock.

"I never told your mother or your grandmother what I was up to. They'd have worried too much. Then later, when Ironwater took over and the city banned plumbers, I figured that was the end of it. And I was fine with that, even relieved. Let somebody else be out there putting their butt on the line, pardon my language. Only it turned out Ironwater wasn't what we thought they were. They charged outrageous prices, cheated their customers. It was wrong. So some of us plumbers did the only thing we could. We formed a resistance."

"P.I.E.," I say.

Big Joe rolls his eyes.

"The name was Tiny's idea. He likes pie."

He laughs. I never thought I'd hear Big Joe laugh like that, or that he'd be sitting here in the kitchen talking to me like a real grandfather. But here he is, telling me about the old days. It feels good, but one thing still bothers me.

"Where have you been for the last four years?"

His smile goes away.

"Moving around, different places," he says, and I can tell from the tone it wasn't because he likes to travel. "I couldn't stay here, not after Ironwater found me."

I gasp. I can't help it. It's like that comic book where Dr. Mayhem pulls the mask off Tarantula Man.

"Ironwater knows who you are?"

Joe nods and looks down at the floor.

"They showed up at my door four years ago and said they wanted me to retire, quit the business, drop out of sight. And if I didn't, they'd go after my friends, my family, anyone I cared about."

"But why didn't they just arrest you, like they did Tank?"

He looks at me and shakes his head.

"You don't understand, boy. They wanted Joe Feeney to retire—not the Midnight Flush."

Only I do understand. A little TV set in my mind starts replaying all those smiling Pepper Hayes news reports that never seemed to make any sense. Well, they made sense now. Ironwater's foolproof plumbing system was failing, and they needed someone to blame. And they couldn't very well blame the Midnight Flush if Big Joe was sitting in a jail cell.

"What happens if they find out you're back?" I ask.

Joe sighs.

"They know I'm back," he says, handing me a slip of paper.

It's the Toilet King picture.

"But how did—"

Joe points to the mirror in the background of the photo. In it is a perfect reflection of his face. I'd never have noticed it in a hundred years. But Ironwater did.

"A couple of Icks brought that by this afternoon, just to let me know they're watching me," he says, and the thought makes my stomach ache.

This is why the Icks were following me, to get to Joe. For all I know, I led them here.

"That's why I took down your posters. I don't want anything in this house tying you to what P.I.E. is doing."

"And what are you doing?" I ask.

Joe gives me a long, probing look, then waves off

the question and leans back in his chair. But just when I think our discussion is over, he rubs his chin.

"Um, there's something I've been meaning to ask you about, boy. This fellow you work with, Max Bleeker..."

Max? He knows about Max? I wonder what other gigantic secrets he's been keeping from me.

"What about him?" I ask.

"Well, what do you think of him? As a person, I mean?"

"He's kind of horrible," I say.

I'm just being honest.

"And what sort of a plumber is he?"

"Amazing," I say, which is also honest.

"Yeah, that's what I've heard," Joe says. "Now, would you say he's the kind of fellow who knows how to do a job professionally and discreetly? I wouldn't want my grandson working with someone irresponsible."

"Oh, don't you worry," I tell him. "Max is totally responsible."

Chapter 21

Saturday, 10:15 a.m.

"Take the wheel," Max says.

Without warning, he stands up and walks to the back of the van. I leap from my seat and grab hold of the steering wheel.

"Max! I don't know how to drive!"

"Relax, you're doing great," he says. "Just don't hit anything. I don't have insurance."

I'm trying to watch the road and, at the same time, keep an eye on Max. What's he doing back there? In the rearview mirror, I see an industrial-sized barrel sitting by the loading doors. That's not unusual; Max carries all kinds of junk around in this dump-on-wheels. Still, there's something odd about it. For one thing, it's moving.

CLANGGGG!

Suddenly, the metal lid flies into the air and bounces off the side of the van. I watch in horror as a slimy pink blob bursts out of the barrel and raises its terrifying flippers.

HONNNNNK!

Oh great, now I'm in the wrong lane! I jerk the van back across the white stripe, flinging Max against the wall.

"Is that a maulrusk?" I ask, the irritation coming through in my voice. "Tell me you don't have us speeding down the freeway with a live maulrusk in the van."

"Shut up and drive," Max says.

If you've never met a maulrusk, congratulations. It's not a pretty sight. Essentially, it's just a gargantuan wad of mucus with two long tusks. They call it a maulrusk because, well, it likes to maul stuff.

"What are you doing with that thing, anyway?" I ask him.

Max locks eyes with the oozy rider, sizing up the competition.

"I'm having a little dispute with my cable company," he says, delivering a hard roundhouse punch to the horrible, jiggling squish.

The squish seems mildly annoyed. Max puts it in a headlock, and the two of them wrestle there in the back of the van—man against blob, terrible creature against terrible creature-in-a-can.

"See, we've got this difference of opinion," he grunts. "They think I should pay my cable bill; I think they should find a big pink squish-monster in their toilet. It's called negotiation."

"That's insane," I tell him.

"I know. Why should I have to pay for channels I don't even watch?"

BRRRRMMP-BRRRRMMP!

I hear a horn-blast from an eighteen-wheeler, and when I check the side mirror, I see the driver shaking his fist at me. Rude. Considering I have no license and no training, I think I'm doing pretty well. I pull the wheel hard and move back across two lanes, sending Max flying into space like an out-of-control astronaut.

He smashes into his toolbox and lets out a loud groan.

"It would've been safer to let the maulrusk drive," he mumbles.

"Sorry!"

Max grabs the metal lid from the van floor and begins forcing the creature back into the can. After a few blows, it sinks back into the barrel, and he seals it inside. He tosses a spare tire on top for good measure.

"Whew," he says, climbing back into his seat and taking the wheel. "That was a close one. By the way, this counts as a driving lesson. You owe me for gas."

I roll my eyes and climb back into my own seat. Max turns on the radio. It's on the sports station, because it's always on the sports station. The changer knob is broken.

"So," he says, "did you ever figure out why those Icks were after you?"

"No," I tell him.

It's not a lie, but it's close. I don't know exactly what the Icks were going to ask me, but I'm pretty sure it had something to do with the Midnight Flush being back in town. But I can't tell Max that without revealing some fairly huge family secrets.

Besides, for all I know, the Icks might not be done with me. They can't be happy with the way our last meeting ended.

"I just wish I knew who was on that motorcycle," I say. "I kind of feel like I ought to pay them or something."

"They got to knock an Ick's teeth out. That's better than getting paid," Max says.

That's kind of true. Nobody likes Icks. They're supposed to be Ironwater's private security force, but what they really are is a goon squad that does their dirty work.

I slouch down in my seat and turn up the basketball game on the radio. A commercial comes on.

"You know, burritos and toilets go together like a basketball and a hoop," a grandfatherly-sounding man says. *"Hi. I'm Herman Wiest, chairman of the Ironwater Corporation. Ironwater is proud to be Nitro City's number one choice for high-quality, high-security toilets. We're also proud to be the official sponsor of the Fiftieth Anniversary Burrito Festival. Opening day is just around the corner, and tickets are going fast, so—"*

Max shuts off the radio.

"It's going to be big this year," I say. "Should be a lot of fun. Are you going?"

"Can't. I'm allergic," he says.

"To burritos?"

He shakes his head.

"Fun."

Chapter 22

Monday, 4:05 p.m.

I'm sitting in Griddle Buns waiting for Nixon in our regular booth, the one in the back with no exposed rear flank.

He's late, of course. Probably got detention again. I grab my phone and check for a message. While I'm scrolling through my texts, I hear the red vinyl seat make a squeaking sound across from me.

It's Izzy Cisco.

"You're not Nixon," I tell her.

"And I thank God for that every day," she says. "What are you doing?"

"Enjoying the solitude. Well, I *was*," I say, checking my phone.

Izzy is wearing a long-sleeve black T-shirt, a silver bracelet, white sunglasses, and a smile. The smile doesn't exactly look evil, but we both know it is.

"So, still being chased by—what did you call them? Icks?"

I shrug.

"I've been thinking," she says. "What would an Ick want with you? For that matter, what would anyone want with you?"

I grit my teeth.

The truth is, I'm tempted to tell Izzy she's right: the Icks didn't want me, they wanted my grandfather. And thanks to her stupid picture, they found him. But that would only prolong the conversation, adding precious seconds to the amount of time it takes her to go away.

"Anyway, loser," she says, "I wanted to ask—"

"Hi!"

I look up from my phone. April Danvers is standing beside the booth.

"Hey, April."

"Is this a bad time?" she asks. "I don't want to interrupt."

"Oh, you're not interrupting anything. Izzy was just leaving."

"No, I wasn't," Izzy says.

"Well, she will eventually. Would you like to sit down?"

"No, I can't stay," she says. "I just wanted to make sure you're okay. I haven't had a chance to check on you since, well...the incident."

"The incident" is a nice way of saying I got a few gallons of toilet water dumped on me in homeroom.

"I'm fine," I tell her. "But it was awesome of you to ask."

She grins, but I can see something's worrying her.

"Do they think it was that person who's been causing all the bathroom problems?" she says.

"Yeah, it was the Phantom Clogger."

"That's what I thought," she says, then changes to a whisper. "Sully, if I think I know something about that, should I tell someone?"

Wait a minute. April knows something about the Clogger?

"Yes, you should absolutely tell someone," I say,

trying to control the excitement in my voice. "Actually, I've been looking into it myself. You know, sort of as a hobby."

"Me, too!" April says. "I mean, it's just so disgusting, and it's happening right here in our school. Someone's got to stop them."

I nod.

"What do you think you know?"

"Well, remember how someone put a toilet seat in your chair?"

"It rings a bell," I say.

"After that happened, I checked out the upstairs toilet and saw that the seat was missing."

"I saw the same thing."

"And while I was in there," she explains, "I noticed this strange smell."

"I did, too, but I couldn't figure out what it was."

"Heartthrob cologne," she says.

She's right! It was Heartthrob cologne.

"Scott Turbin wears gallons of it," April says.

It all adds up. Scott's scent puts him at the scene of the crime. And from the way he was cracking up about the toilet seat, the odds are pretty good he's the one who put it there.

"I'll check it out, April. But this is good work."

"Oh, not really. I just do a lot of puzzles." She smiles. "See you later."

She starts to leave, then pauses.

"Hey, you want to go to the Burrito Festival together?"

I look around, just to be sure she's talking to me.

"Yeah, that'd be great," I say.

"Awesome. Bye now."

April turns around, and I watch her glide away from the table.

"Hey!" Izzy says.

I look at her.

"Oh, you still here?"

"Yes, I'm still here," she says. Her arms are crossed and her eyebrows are menacing. "So what's the deal with you and April Danvers?"

"There is no deal. We've just talked a couple of times."

She shrugs.

"Sometimes that's all it takes. So do you see a future with her?"

"A future?"

My face squishes up like a leftover jack-o'-lantern.

"Yeah," she says. "I mean, have you guys made other plans? Like, are you going to the prom together?"

"The prom?"

She nods.

"The senior prom?" I say. "The one that happens four years from now?"

She nods again.

"No," I say, trying to shake off the weirdness of this conversation. "I have no plans to go to the senior prom with April."

"Oh, good," she says. "Will you go with me?"

The question hits me like a hard kick under the table, except the kick would be a lot more appealing.

"That's crazy. I'm your archnemesis. Why would you want to go to the prom with me?"

"Oh, I don't," she says. "That's why I'm asking you now."

Okay, I'm totally confused.

"Look, everyone knows the senior prom is filled with drama."

"It is?"

She rolls her eyes.

"Okay, everyone but you. Anyway, it's a well-known

fact that sixty percent of prom-goers will end up dumping their original date to go with someone else."

"Sixty percent?"

"All right, eighty percent, I don't know, but it's a lot," she says. "The point is, the chances are very good that I'm going to end up dumping someone in order to go with someone else. And I'd feel terrible about that!"

"Would you?" I ask.

"Yes, I would. Unless..."

I wait, but she doesn't finish her sentence.

"Unless what?"

"Unless my original date is someone I'd actually enjoy dumping."

"You mean someone like me?" I ask.

"No, no, not someone *like* you. You."

Her eyes burrow into me like they're trying to rip an answer out of my soul. Jeez, I wish Nixon would show up.

"Couldn't this question wait a couple of years?"

Izzy's jaw drops.

"Are you kidding?" she says. "Jenny Pinkman has had her dispose-a-date lined up since fourth grade. Oscar Johnson has already dumped his first choice, and is working on the second one. If anything, I've waited too long. So what's it going to be?"

My stomach feels sick and fluttery, the way it always does when I have to make a decision. I mean, on the one hand, if we did go together, she'd probably have a really rotten time. On the other hand, she might want to dance and stuff.

"I'll have to think about it," I tell her.

She pouts.

"Fine. But if you think you've got a shot at being dumped by someone better than me, you're just delusional."

"I'll keep that in mind."

I expect her to leave, because that's what people usually do when you're ignoring them. Only she doesn't. Also, she's staring.

"So what's it like in the sewer?" she says.

"Excuse me?"

"You hang out there, right? That's why they call you sewer boy."

"*They* don't call me sewer boy. Only you call me sewer boy."

"Okay, that's why *I* call you sewer boy," she says. "But you have been there, right?"

"Why do you want to know?"

"Because I'm doing my term paper on it for history class," she says. "Will you take me the next time you go?"

"What? No!"

"Why not?"

"I don't know, because it would be weird. And because it would mean spending time with you. And trust me, you don't want to go down there anyway. So forget it, I'm not taking you."

"Fine, I'll go by myself."

"Good luck finding a way in," I say.

"Oh, I'll find a way in."

I try to muffle a laugh, but it escapes through my nostrils.

"If you find a way into the Underworld, I'll go to the prom with you."

"Good," she says. "I look forward to dumping you the day before the dance."

Chapter 23

Wednesday, 2:42 p.m.

I reach into the jar on Leonard's desk, but there's not an orange jelly bean in sight. Just green. Every single one of them is yucky, flavorless green.

"What happened to the good ones?" I ask.

"People ate them," Leonard says. "That's how life is, Sully. Other people get the good stuff, and you have to make do with what's left."

Leonard is in one of his moods.

I wrinkle my nose and push the horrible bean

through my unwilling lips. Nothing green tastes good. It's the color of phlegm and vegetables.

"All right, you wanted this meeting, so let's get down to business," he says. "Tell me about the Phantom Clogger."

"Well, I've got this new lead…"

Leonard throws his hands into the air.

"Another lead?"

"Wait, this one's promising—"

"You keep telling me that, and yet Mr. Krumsky keeps having to mop up your failures! I need results, Sully. Not promises. If you can't—"

I toss three cigarette butts onto his desk. He hits me with a long, frustrated eye roll.

"Torpedoes? Really, Torpedoes?"

Leonard yanks out his top drawer and turns it upside down. Dried-up old cigarettes fall like snowflakes.

"In the past three months, I've seen more Torpedoes than the US Navy. You can stop bringing me every butt you fish out of a toilet."

"These aren't from a toilet," I tell him. "I found them in a locker."

Leonard's eyes widen, and the blood rushes out of his face. He leans forward.

"Give me a name, Sully."

I stare him in the pupils.

"Scott Turbin."

Leonard swallows hard, and I see him steady himself on the back of a chair. He looks visibly shaken.

"Scott Turbin? He's an honor student. And the best-smelling kid in school."

"I know. That's what put me on his trail."

I tell him about the Heartthrob cologne, and the missing toilet seat that somehow ended up in my chair just before the ceiling collapsed.

"I believe the Phantom was targeting me. That means he had to know where I sit. Scott's in my homeroom. Also, whoever it was had to get here early enough to set everything up. Scott comes in at six fifteen on Thursdays for Glee Club practice. The pieces fit. Then, when I checked his locker, I found the Torpedoes."

"Scott Turbin," Leonard mutters, shaking his head. "We've got to be sure, Sully. We can't afford to make a mistake. I'll get him in here, work him a little, maybe he'll tell me the truth."

"He won't," I say. "Scott's not the type to crack. Let me stay on him, see if I can't catch him in the act. I think that's our best shot."

Leonard nods.

"All right, we'll do it your way. But do it fast. We've spent too much time on the Clogger already, and there's something else I need you to look into."

"What?"

"A noise," he says. "It sounds like it's coming from the pipes in the second-floor boys' room. It's probably nothing, but with all the problems happening around the district, I don't want to take any chances."

"Got it," I say.

I swivel on my heels and head toward Leonard's door.

"Oh, Sully, there's one more thing you should know," he says. "Scott Turbin was in my office today... he's the one who ate the last orange jelly bean."

My jaw tightens, and my hands ball themselves into fists. I'm coming for you, Scott. And this time, it's personal.

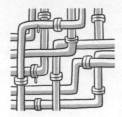

Chapter 24

Saturday, 4:23 p.m.

"Hi, honey!"

My mom's supernaturally happy face is on my computer. There's something disturbing on top of her head.

"So…what do you think?" she asks.

For the most part, it looks like she's wearing an ordinary blue baseball cap. But I can't ignore the long, hovering spatula sticking out of the front of it.

"Isn't it fun? We call it the 'hatula'! It's the best spatula promotion we've ever come up with," she says.

"Wow! That's…" I grit my teeth and force the word out between them. "Awesome."

She beams.

"It was all my idea," she says. "I was thinking, what can we do to keep spatulas on a customer's mind? Answer—put one on their head!"

"Amazing," I say.

"I know! But listen to me, going on and on about spatula hats. Which I guess proves my point—people can't stop talking about them! But that's not the reason I called. Is your grandfather around? Because I have big news!" Mom says, her head-spatula rising with pride.

"No, he's not here right now. What's the news?"

"Oh, it's fantastic! Come here, Phil!"

She motions to my dad, and he walks onto the screen and sits down beside her.

"Hi, son!" he says.

There he is, smiling and waving and wearing a bright-red hatula. The imprint on the front says NITRO CITY BURRITO FESTIVAL.

Mom claps her hands.

"Isn't that incredible? You can print words directly onto the hat! We made up a whole bunch of them to give away at the Burrito Festival. Everybody will be talking about them!"

"I'll bet," I say.

"But that's not the big news. The big news is that they've asked your father to write a poem for the festival this year."

"Aw, it's no big deal," Dad says.

"No big deal? It's a huge honor!" Mom tells him. "You're finally being recognized for your contributions to culinary poetry."

"Well, I do like to rhyme stuff with food," he says.

A half grin shows up on his face.

"Go ahead. Read Sully what you've come up with."

"Okay," he says. "Now, it's just a work in progress, so don't expect too much."

He picks up a piece of paper and clears his throat.

"'Ode to a Burrito,'" he says.

"With meat, and beans, and rolled tortilla,
You give us joy, and diarrhea—"

"Stop!" I yell.

"I know! I know! But it's impossible," Dad explodes. "You try coming up with a rhyme for 'tortilla.'"

"What about 'Nice to see ya'?"

"'See ya'! Of course!"

He lets out a loud, injured groan, and pounds his head against the coffee table.

"Stop that, dear, you'll bend your spatula," Mom says. "So what about you, Sully? Are you excited about the festival?"

I shrug.

"Sure, I guess."

"It's the fiftieth anniversary," Mom says. "You and Nixon are going to have so much fun."

"I'm, uh, not going with Nixon this year. See, there's this girl—"

"A girl!" she squeals.

"Mom, it's not like that. Her name is April Danvers, and we both just like burritos."

My mom's face is glowing, and she waves her finger at me.

"Oh, don't tell me this is just about the burritos. After all, the Burrito Festival isn't just a food thing, it's filled with—"

"Failure and disappointment," my dad moans.

"Don't listen to him, he's just in one of his funks," Mom says. "Wait a minute, I've got an idea. Does April have a favorite color?"

"I don't know, she wears a lot of pink."

Her smile looks like it's going to explode.

"Well, guess who's going to be getting their own pink hatula!"

My mom is amazing. Eight thousand miles away, and she can still totally ruin my life.

"Oh, boy," I say. "I'll warn...I mean, *tell* her."

Chapter 25

Saturday, 8:27 p.m.

The little bell rings when I walk into the Golden Poo, and I look up at the sign that warns you about the tinkle. It's funnier now that I know this is a plumber's dive.

"Well, if it isn't the golden child," Tank Huberman says. "What brings you here, Sully?"

"I thought I'd try another chili burger," I tell him.

"You sure you can handle it?"

I nod. "What doesn't kill us makes us stronger."

Tiny Dinkins laughs so hard he nearly falls off his stool.

"One chili burger, comin' up," Tank says. "You want an egg cream with that?"

"What's an egg cream?"

He gives me the scientific formula, but what it comes down to is this: an egg cream is a sweet, fizzy drink that doesn't have eggs, and doesn't have cream. The mystery is too intriguing to pass up.

I find Big Joe sitting on the same barstool he was riding last week. If there's a hello in his mouth, it doesn't come out. He picks up a French fry, sucks on it for a minute, then flings it onto the counter.

"What are you doing?" I say.

"I don't like fries," he tells me.

"Then why did you order them?"

"I like the ketchup," he says.

I can't argue with that. I mean, what's he supposed to do, drink it straight out of the bottle?

I turn around and check out the room. It's crowded tonight, including some faces I don't recognize from before. But that's not the only thing that's changed. A week ago, Big Joe was a conquering hero. Today, he's just a guy with greasy fingers and way too much on his mind. I don't know what's worrying him, but it looks like it weighs a ton.

"Is something wrong?" I ask.

"Wrong? What could be wrong? I'm sitting here in a greasy spoon swapping old plumber stories, and the Burrito Festival is two weeks away."

"I know, I can't wait! It's the fiftieth anniversary this year. Aren't you excited?"

"Whoopee," he grunts.

I've heard more enthusiasm come out of a head of lettuce.

"Have you got a problem with the Burrito Festival, Big Joe?"

He shakes his head. Tiny Dinkins swivels on his stool to face us.

"It's not the festival," Tiny says. "It's what comes after the festival."

After? What does he mean by "after"?

"The flushes, son," Tank says. "The flushes."

I look at Big Joe. He's sitting there filling his guts with ketchup and dread. That's when it hits me—the real reason he came back to Nitro City.

It's the Burrito Festival.

People come from everywhere for the festival. It's

a huge event, and this year is supposed to shatter all records. And not just attendance records.

Flushes per hour, flushes per day, flushes per toilet, flushes per person, volume, weight, mass, density, frequency…

When this thing's over, Nitro City will hold them all.

"The system can't handle the stress," Joe says. "And when it fails—heaven help us."

My eyes are as wide as manhole covers.

"But Ironwater says—"

"Ironwater thinks their blasted technology is going to hold! But it won't. It's already starting to break down," he says.

He's right. Leonard told me there are plumbing problems at every school in the city. And I've personally seen the size of the creatures that crawl into people's houses. Add in the news reports about major collapses supposedly caused by P.L.U.N.G.E., and you've got the makings of a disaster.

"Ironwater's gizmos and gadgets won't stop what's coming," Joe says. "Every plumber—every real plumber—knows we've only got one shot: Merv."

"Who's Merv?" I ask.

M.E.R.V., it turns out, is the Master Emergency Release Valve. Joe says the plumbers built it decades ago as a last-chance, do-or-die, catastrophe-avoiding reset of the entire sewer system.

"So why don't you just use that?" I ask.

He lets out a loud sigh and slumps on his stool.

"Because it's under that stinkin' dome."

The Nitrodome?

This is bad. The Nitrodome is an impenetrable fortress, no way in and no way out. Whatever's locked away beneath it—and according to rumor, that's some pretty terrifying stuff—is meant to be locked away forever.

"Give it up, Joe. It's hopeless," Tiny says.

"It's not hopeless!" Joe snaps. "Not as long as we've got Merv. And if we can just get someone into the dome..."

"How?" asks Tank. "Are we going to build a giant drill and burrow into the earth? Are we going to get a super-magnet and yank it out of the ground? Face it, Joe, we're plumbers. We don't know anything about breaking into high-security mega-domes."

I put down my chili burger and stare at Tank. Because he's absolutely right—plumbers don't know the first thing about how to break into impenetrable, high-tech mega-domes.

But I know someone who might.

Chapter 26

Monday, 3:44 p.m.

After school, I enter the Underworld through a manhole behind the old abandoned Thirty-Eighth Street amusement park. The cover looks like it's sealed, but if you get under it with a pry bar, it pops right up.

I head down a long, winding passage. At the far end of the tunnel, glowing red eyes flicker in the shadows. It's probably sewer rats; they're everywhere down here. After a while, they become like ugly wallpaper—just part of the background. You get used to—

"Eeeeeee-hee-hee-hee-hee-hee-hee!"

Uh-oh. That was no sewer rat. The high-pitched laugh echoes through the shaft, and the sound crawls over my skin like a million spiders. There's a second laugh, and a third, and a fourth. And then a long, terrifying howl.

Suddenly, something fast and wild-looking streaks at me out of the darkness. It's...it's...

"Run!"

It's Izzy Cisco.

Behind her is a pack of laughing byenas. If you've never seen one, a byena looks a lot like a hyena, except it's bigger, meaner, and has two heads. That's right, two heads—which means one can laugh at you while the other one eats your face.

"I can't believe you followed me!" I yell.

"Well, I wouldn't have had to if you'd brought me like I asked!" she yells back.

We race down a side tunnel and manage to put some distance between us and the pack. I'm not sure where the nearest exit is, but I'm determined to find it fast. The sewer might be the size of the city, but there's no way I'm sharing it with Izzy. I make a quick turn down an alleyway, and she tries to follow me.

"Owwwwwww!" she yells.

"What happened?"

"I think I twisted my ankle."

Oh, perfect. I help her to her feet, then hear the howl of a byena coming down the tunnel. We'll never make it out.

"This way," I say.

Izzy's limp slows us down, but we finally reach the spot: a stretch of wall that looks just like every other stretch of wall.

I whirl around and press my hands against the concrete.

"What are you doing?" Izzy asks.

I don't answer. My palms move up and down and across in a desperate search. Where is it? I hear another howl, and a bloodcurdling laugh.

"They're coming!" she says.

I force myself not to panic. My hands are a blur as they tear at the wall, because it's gotta be here, it's just gotta. I feel Izzy grab my shoulder.

"Sully!"

Just a couple more seconds, that's all I need, and...

There's a click, and a creak, and the wall opens.

"Whoaaaaaaa!" Izzy gasps. "How did you do that?"

I'd tell her, but I'm not real sure myself. The truth is, I got lucky.

"Come on," I say.

We walk down the narrow alley and stop in front of the heavy steel door.

"What is this place?" she says.

"A friend of mine lives here."

"You have sewer friends?" she says, scrunching up her nose.

I ignore her and bang on the door. I have to, because there's no doorbell—the Moleman doesn't get a lot of visitors. Or want them. A terrible thought crosses my mind. I'm knocking on the secret entrance to a super-villain's underground lair—what if we're about to be scalded with acid, or fried by a laser?

I step behind Izzy.

"Moleman?" I yell. "Moleman, it's me, Sullivan!"

There's no answer.

I knock again.

"It's Sullivan Stringfellow, Moleman! I'm sorry, I know I shouldn't have come here, but it was an emergency!"

Still no answer. I look at Izzy, but she's not looking

at me. She's just staring at the door. She takes a couple of steps toward it and knocks.

"Hello? Hello?" she calls. "It's Isabelle. Open the door, Uncle Victor."

Uncle Victor?

I hear a beeping noise, then a sound like air rushing out of an inner tube, and the door slides open.

Standing in front of us is the Moleman. His face looks like it always does, but his eyebrows seem more villainous than usual.

"Ah, company," he says. "What a delightful invasion of privacy."

Chapter 27

Monday, 4:37 p.m.

"The Moleman is your uncle?"

"Great uncle, actually. On my mom's side."

"Yes, Isabelle's mother is a lawyer. An honest one. I blame myself," the Moleman says. "Come inside, children."

We do.

"Wow!" Izzy says.

Apparently, this is her first visit to the Moleman's lair.

"Oh, I think we can do better than this," the Mole-man says.

He pushes a button, and a metal door slides open. We step through it.

"Wow," I say.

There's a whole house in here. He's got a couch made out of an old bombshell, chairs that look like they could electrocute you, a ceiling fan made of swords, a lamp with a glowing skull, a pool table where every ball is the eight ball, and a banjo—the ultimate instrument of torture.

"What are you doing here, Isabelle?" the Moleman says.

He doesn't look happy.

"I wanted to see you," she says. "We were worried. We haven't heard from you. I didn't know how to get in touch, so I took a chance and followed sewer boy down here."

"Yes, I see," the Moleman says. "I'm afraid I have been neglectful. It's just that I've been working on... something."

I'm pretty ticked off that Izzy lied to me, but I guess I can understand why.

Anyway, if she hadn't followed me, I'd never have gotten to see this amazing room. My eyes dart around and land on an old photograph on the wall. It's the Moleman standing next to a tall, lean figure in a black mask and a yellow Spandex bodysuit.

"You knew the Human Waste?" I say.

He nods.

"He used to have a lair not far from here. In the old days, there were lairs all over the Underworld. But then P.L.U.N.G.E. started snooping around and, well, there goes the neighborhood."

Wow. The Golden Age must have been something.

"I just read a rumor that the Human Waste is back," I say. "Crazy, huh?"

The Moleman thinks for a second, then shrugs.

"Of course it's crazy," I tell him. "He's dead. You remember, they found his body in the sewer."

"Yes, I remember them finding a body," he says. "And it was wearing H.W.'s suit. But that's the thing about Spandex, isn't it? One size fits all."

Izzy narrows her eyes.

"You think it might have been somebody else?"

"Oh, I have no idea," the Moleman says. "It's just that I distinctly remember that in their final battle, the

Midnight Flush bit H.W. just below the knee. It left a nasty scar. And yet, I've heard this body had no scars whatsoever. But perhaps my sources are unreliable."

A tingle climbs up my backbone. He's messing with us, right? I'm too young to remember the Human Waste's reign of terror, but the stories are legendary. He came within inches of not only controlling the sewer, but destroying the city.

"Are you all right, Sullivan?"

"Fine," I gulp.

We take a place on the couch, and the Moleman sits in one of the more comfortable-looking electric chairs. He looks at me.

"So, I know why Isabelle is here, but what brings you to the Underworld today?" he says.

"Actually, I was coming to see you. I wanted to ask about the Nitrodome."

The Moleman crosses his legs.

"What about it?"

"How would you get into it?" I ask.

He gives me a long, curious stare.

"What are you up to, Sullivan?"

"That's sort of a secret," I tell him.

I see a very small grin.

"A secret, eh? I trust this is for some evil purpose?"

"Oh, the evilest," I assure him.

The Moleman rubs his chin and lifts one eyebrow.

"Well, I wish I could help you, Sullivan. But the truth is, the Nitrodome is impenetrable. Getting inside is absolutely impossible."

"Impossible?"

"Impossible," he says.

My stomach sinks. I mean, this is the Moleman, the twisted genius who invented the toilet-paper flamethrower. He's the brain behind some of the most diabolical creations in supervillainy. I never thought he'd just give up on the ultimate challenge. But maybe it really is impossible.

The disappointment oozes out of me, and I slouch down in my seat. Izzy glances at me, then turns her eyes to the Moleman.

"That's okay, Uncle Victor. If you say you can't get in, then you can't get in," she says. "Sully, I guess you'll just have to go with that other plan."

"Other plan?" I say.

"Yes. The *other* plan," she says, staring at me so hard I can feel her pupils drilling into my brain. "You know, the one you *told* me about?"

The Moleman cocks his head.

"What's she talking about, Sullivan?"

I pause a second, asking myself that very question. And then it hits me.

"Oh, right. The *other* plan," I say. "Yeah, I guess we'll just go ahead and use that one. Dr. Sludge seemed pretty sure about it."

"Sludge?" the Moleman says. "You've been in touch with Sludge?"

"Uh-huh," I say.

Honestly, I wouldn't know Thaddeus Sludge if I ran into him on the street. But I do know he was an evil scientist back during the Golden Age, and his rivalry with the Moleman is legendary.

"What's Sludge's plan?" he asks.

"I'm afraid that's a secret," Izzy tells him.

"Right," I say. "Still, you've got to hand it to him. It takes a truly evil mind to figure out how to do something that even the once-brilliant Moleman admits is impossible."

"What do you mean *once* brilliant?" he says.

"I meant it as a compliment," I say. "I don't care what anybody says, you used to be brilliant. Just because you've slipped a little with age…"

"I have never slipped, and I never will."

"Sorry," I tell him. "I just meant that some things might be a little advanced for you. Like the Nitrodome."

The Moleman's face hardens like a drying sponge.

"Of course, when I said impossible, I meant impossible for you," he says. "If I put my mind to it, I'm sure I could come up with something."

"Dr. Sludge has already put his mind to it," Izzy says.

The Moleman's long, bony fingers clench into a fist.

"Oh, what was I thinking?" he says. "There is something I've been tinkering with that could be just what you're looking for. It completely slipped my mind."

"Can we see it?" Izzy says.

The Moleman gives her an odd look.

"Well, I suppose at some point we might..."

"What about now?" she says. "I'd love to see what my favorite uncle is up to."

The Moleman's eyes widen. He turns to me.

"Yeah, what about now?" I say.

The double-team is wearing him down. He slumps his shoulders and leans against the back of the electric chair.

"All right." He sighs. "I'll get my cloak."

Chapter 28

Monday, 6:02 p.m.

Now, this is the way to travel.

We're in the Mole-mobile, the Moleman's legendary super-car. It was custom-made for him forty years ago, but it will never go out of style. It's silver and black, with tall tail fins in the back shaped like demon wings. The front has a retractable drill, and there are at least a dozen buttons inside I'm not allowed to touch under any circumstance, except for an alien invasion.

It is one sweet ride.

I have never ridden in the Mole-mobile before. I

didn't even know it still existed, but today I'm getting my chance for the last reason I would've ever expected: the Moleman's secret dome-buster is not in the sewer.

This absolutely floors me. Who knew the Moleman ever left the Underworld? I've always thought of him as being kind of like Count Dracula—you know, having to avoid daylight at all costs. But I guess I was wrong.

So does this mean he does other regular-person stuff, too? I'm trying to imagine him getting haircuts and going to the supermarket. Sure, it'd probably be an evil supermarket, but still…the thought of him buying socks and fabric softener and pushing around the little cart is almost more than I can handle.

"Thanks for bringing us out here, Uncle Victor," Izzy says. "I hope we didn't push you into it."

"No, no, it's fine," the Moleman tells her. "Like I always say, what's the point of building a secret weapon if you can't show it off?"

We pull up in front of a large, plain-looking warehouse building. The Moleman takes the padlock off the door, and we go inside.

"What is this place?" I say.

"Just something I keep for...special projects," he says. "Follow me."

We walk down a short hallway and stop at a small office. There's a workbench with several strange-looking devices on it.

"Is this the one?" Izzy asks.

She's holding something that looks like a super-advanced toilet plunger, possibly from the future.

"No, no, that's the Party Pooper 3000. It's, uh...not finished."

"What is it?"

The Moleman looks embarrassed.

"Well, it was supposed to be the ultimate party prank. I mean, what's funnier than an exploding toilet plunger, right?" he says. "Let's say some party pooper is dragging down your gathering, and you want to get rid of them. All you have to do is tell them the toilet's clogged, ask them to plunge it, and then—boom! You've popped your pooper. Classic bathroom humor. The only problem is, I made it too powerful, and—well, you know what they say: there's a thin line between comedy and tragedy. It's much too dangerous to keep at the lab."

Izzy carefully puts it back on the table and eases away.

"Which one of these is for getting into the dome?" I ask.

"These? None of them," he says.

"Then why are we here?"

He reaches into a desk drawer and pulls out a black remote control that looks like a TV channel changer.

"For this," he says.

We walk down the hall to the rear of the warehouse, which is a room approximately the size of Kentucky. The Moleman pushes a button on the remote control. Huge overhead lights flicker, and one by one, they turn on.

Then he pauses. But there's nothing there.

"This isn't one of those imaginary inventions, is it?" I say. "Because you could've shown us that in the sewer."

The Moleman lets out a long, sad sigh.

"Thank you for killing the suspense, Sullivan."

He lifts the remote and clicks. Slowly, the floor opens up, and out of it rises one of the wonders of our age.

"Wowwwwwwwwww!"

It is the single largest toilet bowl on the face of the Earth.

"I call it the Death Flush," he says. "It's the size of an Olympic swimming pool, holds 612,000 gallons of water, and is capable of administering the most powerful flush ever known to man."

"This is awesome!" I yell, because I can't help myself. "How does it work?"

The Moleman grins. It's like he's been waiting for me to ask.

"When activated, the Death Flush begins generating a massive cyclo-toiletronic swirl, which, at maximum power, will produce enough speed and pressure to rocket a single human being through the pipeline, past the safeguards, and directly into the dome."

"So you flush them like a poo," Izzy says.

We glare at her. Some people just don't get science.

"I'm sorry I doubted you, Moleman," I say. "This is amazing—there really is a way into the Nitrodome."

"Well, yes—and no. Mostly no," he says.

"What do you mean?"

"It isn't finished. By my calculations, it's going to take another year before it's even ready for testing. And I'm not letting a person anywhere near it until

I've flushed a few frogs or goldfish. I'm evil, but I'm not unsafe."

"Well, what if I helped you?" I say. "Could we have it ready in time for the Burrito Festival?"

"The Burrito Festival?" he says, his eyeballs nearly popping out of his face. "Are you out of your mind? It's impossible. It would take an army of plumbers working around the clock to even come close."

I stare up at the big porcelain idol and nod.

"You're right, Moleman. It would take an army."

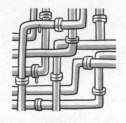

Chapter 29

Wednesday, 4:10 p.m.

I knock on the heavy steel door of the warehouse, but when there's no answer, I go inside.

"Moleman?"

He doesn't respond, but at least now I know why. There's a loud, high-pitched whine coming from a drill in the back part of the building. I walk down the long hallway until I reach the enormous room that holds the Death Flush. The Moleman is hard at work on a metal brace.

"Sullivan?" he calls. "This is a surprise."

He's wearing a pair of black coveralls, a striped tie, and thick protective goggles.

"I wanted to talk to you about that," I say, pointing to the giant toilet towering over us like a flushable King Kong.

"Go on," the Moleman says.

"Well, you said it would take an army to finish it before the Burrito Festival."

I put two fingers in my mouth and whistle. Suddenly, a long, long line of frowning, pudgy, gray-haired plumbers wander into the warehouse. They're holding lunch pails and toolboxes.

"So I brought you one," I say.

At first, I think the Moleman might faint, or maybe have a heart attack. But that passes pretty quickly. As he stares into the faces of the invading mob, his eyes grow colder and meaner, and then they turn on me.

"Traitor!" he yells.

"Now I know how this looks…"

"You pathetic, backstabbing, treasonous insect. I share with you the gifts of my genius, and you bring my mortal enemies down on top of me? *Out!*"

"If you'll just let me—"

"GET OUT!"

"Leave the kid alone. We don't like this any more than you do."

The voice seems to stun the Moleman. He stops yelling at me, and his head slowly rotates toward the crowd.

"Is that…the Tank?"

I nod cautiously. Moleman crosses the room.

"Well, well, well—Tank Huberman," he says, standing just inches from his old nemesis. "My, the years have been terrible to you."

"Tell me about it," Tank says.

The Moleman almost smiles. He lifts his chin and crosses his arms in front of his chest.

"Do you remember the time I put killer bees in your showerhead?" he says.

"Do you remember the time I made you eat a toilet brush?" Tank says.

This time, the Moleman actually does smile.

"The glory days. Where have they gone?"

"I was trying to tell you that they didn't want to come. They were madder about it than you are," I say. "One of them threatened to rip my lungs out through my nostrils."

"Sorry," Big Joe says.

"But in the end, they understood that it's the only way. I mean, do you want to see this whole town destroyed?"

"Of course," the Moleman says, giving me a puzzled look.

"I mean by someone else."

He bites his lower lip.

"You make a good point. But it'll never work."

"Why not?" I say. "These guys are good."

"Exactly."

"What do you mean?"

"They're *good*," the Moleman says. "How are they supposed to build an evil machine?"

There's an anxious rumble in the crowd. Big Joe steps forward.

"We're plumbers. To us, a toilet's a toilet," he says. "It's not how you build it that makes it good or bad. It's what you do with it."

We all stand there in silence. My nerves are stretched as tight as Tiny Dinkins's underwear. The Moleman puts his hands behind his back and takes a slow, methodical walk in front of the row of intruders. His face looks like he just sucked a lemon.

"Helping P.L.U.N.G.E. goes against everything I

stand for," he says, pausing to build the suspense. "But if I don't do it, that means I'm helping Ironwater…so you see my dilemma?"

"Oh absolutely," says Big Joe.

The Moleman makes another march down the line of plumbers.

"All right, I'm in!"

A massive cheer bursts from the crowd.

"But in exchange," the Moleman says, raising his hand, "you will give me complete control over the Nitro City Underworld."

"No."

"All right then, a pizza party."

"Done," says Joe.

Chapter 30

Friday, 9:15 p.m.

Dear Diary: Today I worked on a giant toilet—with actual giants!

I'm kidding—I don't even keep a diary, but if I did, that's what it would say. Because I just spent the last few hours working alongside the giants of plumbing. To see them in action was amazing. These guys are true artists. Now I know what it must've been like to watch Michelangelo work on a toilet.

The whole tired, dirty crew is gathered here at the Poo for chili burgers and egg creams.

"So, you're like a friend of the Moleman?" Tank says.

"I was," I tell him. "But after today, I think I'm off his trusted list."

"You're better off," Joe says. "The guy's a wacka-doodle. But that toilet of his…"

Tank lets out a long, impressed whistle.

"Was that the most beautiful thing you've ever seen?"

"For the first time in my life, I actually felt tiny," says Tiny Dinkins, blotting his eyes with his sleeve. "Sorry, I promised myself I wouldn't cry."

Tank moves in close to the counter and leans on his elbows.

"Well, I guess that brings us to the big question, Joe—who's going down the super pooper?"

Big Joe runs a paw through his thick gray hair.

"You know, I've been thinking about that. I've been thinking about it a lot," he says.

Then he stands up and faces the crowd of the Poo's regulars. He takes off his shoe and bangs it on the counter.

"Quiet down, quiet down!" he hollers. "I've got an announcement to make."

The gang at the Golden Poo falls silent.

"Now, as you know, this particular establishment is the regular haunt of the finest collection of plumbers ever to strap on a tool belt," he says.

The room explodes with hoots and whistles. Joe holds up his hands and the place quiets back down.

"Watching you work on that big, beautiful toilet today was a real pleasure. It reminded me of all the things we used to do," he says. "But it also reminded me that we don't do those things anymore."

A murmur rumbles through the crowd. Where is he going with this?

"Look, I know it's tough. Some of us are getting old, and we're tired of doing the dirty work. The cards are stacked against us, and we need some help."

He pauses, looking around at the silent faces.

"Which is why I want to bring in Max Bleeker."

Did he just say Max Bleeker?

The reaction is instant and ugly, and I'm not just talking about mine. It's like a volcano erupted in here, only instead of lava, it spews swear words.

"Max Bleeker?" Tank yells. "For crying out loud, Joe! The man's insane!"

If you've ever wondered at what point a crowd turns

into a mob, this is it. Everyone is yelling at once, people are pumping their fists in the air, and the only reason they're not trashing the place is that it was pretty much trashed when they got here.

Joe bangs his shoe on the counter again.

"Listen to me!" he yells. "If this plan is going to work, someone has gotta be whirled around in the Moleman's giant toilet and rocketed down a sewer pipe. Then, if they're not dead already, they'll have to fight their way through the Nitrodome. Look around—who am I going to send? You? *You?*"

But his words are swallowed up by the rioting. From what I can make out, Max has locked horns with half the people in here, and he's been extremely rude to the rest.

Things are getting ugly, and I'm kind of looking for a semi-clean place to hide. But then I notice an odd stirring in the back of the room. Slowly, the crowd splits like two sides of a walnut shell. A slim, black-haired woman with a leather jacket and a patch over her eye strolls through the opening. From the way she moves, you'd think she owned the place.

She turns and gives the pack a long, cool glare.

"You guys really want to know about Max Bleeker?" she says.

The effect is amazing. No one makes a sound. I couldn't make one if I wanted to—I can barely breathe. Because it's her...it's One-Eyed Lily Cruz!

"Max Bleeker is a selfish, thoughtless, lying, pathetic, cheating, low-down, miserable excuse for a human being," she says. "But when it comes to this kind of stuff? He's the best there is."

It's like a scene from a movie where the beautiful stranger wins over the angry mob, and they erupt into a chorus of cheers. Only this isn't a movie, there's no cheering, and the mob looks angrier than ever.

Lily shrugs.

"Did I mention there's like zero chance he'll survive?"

Okay, *now* the crowd is cheering. Someone fires up the jukebox, and a couple of people dance, but after a minute everyone tires out and goes back to their burgers.

Lily Cruz strolls toward the counter and stops right in front of us. She looks up at Tank.

"Hello, Tank."

"Hello, Lily," Tank says.

"Who's going to talk to Max?"

Tank glances at Joe.

"The boy," Joe says.

Lily turns and gives me a quiet grin. My knees melt.

"You got a name?"

"Sully," I squeak.

My heart is pounding like a jackhammer.

"Well, Sully. How do you know Max?"

"He's my boss."

She looks surprised.

"I always thought Max worked alone. Do you know him very well?"

"Does anybody?"

Lily's grin widens.

"Good point," she says. "So, from what you've seen, do you think he'll be interested in joining this merry band of misfits?"

"I don't know," I tell her. "Max isn't much of a joiner. But that's probably because nobody ever asks him."

Lily closes her good eye and shakes her fabulous head.

"Here's what you do. Tell him they want him. No... tell him they *need* him," she says. "Only don't tell him I told you to say that."

"Huh?" I ask.

She smiles at me, then spins on the heel of her boot and walks away. Every eye follows her as she glides out the door.

"Is that the girl from the poster? The one with the leather pants?" Joe asks me.

I nod.

"Plumbers sure have changed while I've been away." Tank puts his elbows on the counter.

"How soon do you think you can talk to Bleeker?" he asks.

"I'm seeing him tomorrow. I'll ask him then," I say.

"Good," Big Joe says. "I don't know if Bleeker's the answer, but there's no denying we could use some fresh blood. Just do your best, boy, sort of feel him out on the subject. See where he stands."

"I can do that."

"Sure you can," he says. "But remember, it has to be a secret. Everything depends on our ability to stay in the shadows. No one can know about us."

Chapter 31

Saturday, 3:38 p.m.

"You mean those old weirdos who meet down at the Golden Poo?" Max says. "Sure, everybody knows about them."

"They do?"

"Oh, yeah," he says, giving the rusty old clothes dryer a hard kick. "They get together, swap old plumber stories. They've even got a secret password: *pie*. Can you believe it? I mean, it's a restaurant. There's a pretty good chance pie is going to come up in the conversation."

I don't know why Max is criticizing P.I.E. I mean, what's he doing right now? Hanging out in a dumpy old laundromat looking for stupid mutated weasels.

CLANG!

A washer lid opens and closes, and Max slams a black rubber mallet on top of it.

"Take it easy, Max!" Sleazy Ray says. "You're supposed to be smashing mutants, not my washing machines!"

"Smashing these washers would be doing you a favor," Max says. "How old are these things?"

"They're classics," Sleazy Ray says.

"They're junk."

Generally speaking, Max doesn't have a lot of use for old things—machines, traditions, people—but he's right about these washers. They are pretty junky. Then again, so is everything in this place, including Sleazy Ray. The best I can say about him is that he looks exactly like somebody who'd have a name like Sleazy—scrawny face, greasy hair, and a teeny-tiny mustache that I think he drew on with a pencil. I don't know why Max keeps doing business with him. Every time we come here, he tries to cheat us.

"Just go easy on the equipment, that's all I'm asking," Ray says.

CLANG!

Max brings the hammer down on another washer. This time, there wasn't even a weasel.

We're at the Cleanie Genie Super Premium Laundromat, which looks sort of like a landfill, only dirtier. We came for the same reason we always come here— washer weasels. Ray's machines are so old they don't even have basic safety protection. Which means they wouldn't stand up to an Ironwater inspection, and that's why he calls Max.

There are about thirty ancient washers lined up in two long rows on each side of the aisle. The plan is simple: Max takes one side, I take the other, and whenever a washer weasel's disgusting head pops up...

CLANG!

We smack it with a rubber hammer.

"Dang!" I say. "Missed him."

To be honest, I've always thought they should come up with something better to call these things than "washer weasels." I mean, it's accurate—they're sewer weasels with an odd fondness for washing machines—but the name makes them sound harmless. They're not.

Trust me on this.

"Over there!" I yell.

Max races down the aisle just as one of the lids is starting to lift. It slams back down a second before he gets there. I'll bet if I stuck my head inside a washer right now, I'd hear mocking weasel laughter echoing through the pipes.

"Max, I need to ask you something," I say.

He gives me a suspicious look.

"Is it about a raise?"

"No."

"Then ask away," he says.

I clear my throat.

"You know how we were talking about those plumbers who meet down at the Poo? Well, some of them are living legends," I remind him. "They're the ones who made the Golden Age golden."

"Say no more," Max says. "Who do I make the check out to? Old Plumbers Retirement Home?"

"Will you just listen?" I bark. "You may not know this, but P.L.U.N.G.E. is still a pretty amazing organization. Well, they had a meeting and they've asked me to formally invite you to join their group."

"Seriously?" Max says.

"Seriously."

"And this is a formal invitation?"

I nod.

"Well in that case, I formally reply that I'd rather set my hair on fire," he says.

CLANG!

He swings at another weasel.

"Wait, you haven't heard the best part," I tell him. "They want to send you into the dome."

Max eyeballs me.

"The dome? The Nitrodome?"

I nod.

"And how, exactly, am I supposed to get in there?"

"They flush you down a toilet."

He whacks another washer.

"It's not a regular toilet," I say. "It's called the Death Flush."

"Is that supposed to be a selling point?"

"It's a giant toilet, Max," I say. "A giant toilet is every plumber's dream."

He ignores me.

"If you don't do this, the entire plumbing system could collapse," I tell him.

Max brings the hammer down hard on a washer lid.

"Then business should really pick up."

I stop and shoot him a long, serious stare.

"I wasn't supposed to tell you this, but One-Eyed Lily Cruz was there. A bunch of the plumbers didn't want you, but she got up in front of them and said that you're the best. She said to tell you they need you."

Max's jaw tightens and his head slumps forward. He leans against the side of a washer.

"Lily said that?"

I nod.

"Okay, now I'm definitely not doing it."

"Why not?" I yell.

"Because I'm not a sucker!" he says. "Because my dream isn't to be death-flushed. Because I watch out for me, and I don't want to have to babysit a bunch of worn-out old plumbers who are still trying to play superhero. People like that get you killed. This is the way I am, and this is the way I'm staying! So you can tell the great Lily Cruz she's going to have to find that smiley-faced do-gooder somewhere else. Because I ain't that guy."

I just stand there staring at him. I don't know why I'm surprised. It's the first thing he told me when I started the job: *Max looks out for Max.* He couldn't have made it any plainer. But even though I always knew he was a conceited jerk on the outside, I thought if you drilled down deep enough, you'd find something else. But it turns out you don't—there's just more jerkiness.

I close my eyes and let out a sigh. What am I even doing here? I wanted to be a plumber because they were my heroes. But heroes help. Heroes care. Max is no hero. He's just a wrench-jockey in a run-down laundromat playing a monster-sized version of Whac-A-Mole. And I've got better places to be.

"I quit," I say, setting down the hammer.

I didn't say it to stun him, but I think it does. He turns and stares at me.

"I said I quit. I don't want to work with you anymore."

For a second, Max seems to have something caught in his throat, and he's got an almost human look on his face. But it doesn't last.

"If you want to go, then go," he says, his voice as cold as a popsicle. "I work better alone, anyway."

I unfasten my tool belt and walk down the long aisle of washers. Suddenly, the lid next to me opens, and I find myself face-to-face with an eight-legged, saber-toothed, oversized weasel. It lunges at me, its mouth open like a baby bird's at feeding time. I brace myself for the hit, and then...

SPLAT!

Throwing his hammer from the other end of the laundromat, Max nails the creature with a pinpoint shot. I look at him.

"Call it a going-away present," he says.

Chapter 32

Saturday, 7:09 p.m.

Joe is sitting at the counter in the Golden Poo, his pants hanging lower than I think I've ever seen them. Tank puts a basket of fries and a bottle of ketchup in front of him, but he waves them away.

"What's going on?" I ask.

Tank gives me a long sigh.

"We got some news today. Ironwater is bringing in extra security, packing the festival grounds with Icks. And they've all got one job—keeping us out."

"Can they do that?"

"Haven't you heard?" Tiny Dinkins says. "We're a danger to the city."

Big Joe slams a fist on the counter.

"There has to be a way! Someone's gotta be there to hold the line until Bleeker reaches the valve. We have to buy him time!"

I get a sick, sinking feeling in my stomach.

"About that," I say, looking down at my shoes. "Max said no."

I'm not sure what I'm expecting—anger, I guess. Instead, the three of them just stare out into space, barely reacting at all. I guess that's what happens when you hit bottom—there's nowhere left to fall.

"What are we gonna do, Joe?" Tiny asks, but Joe just shakes his head.

"Nothing. We're banned from the festival. Bleeker's out. It's over."

The faces in the room look like they're at a funeral, and in a way, they are. The dream of saving the city is dead.

"You never know, Joe. Maybe it won't be like before," Tank says.

"It'll be worse," Big Joe tells him. "Ten times worse."

I look at them. They both seem to be lost in some distant memory.

"Worse than what?" I ask.

Tank takes off his white paper hat, and lightly rubs the bridge of his nose.

"The war, kid," he says. "The war."

I sit on my barstool listening to the old sewer soldiers tell the story of the darkest day in the history of Nitro City plumbing.

"It was thirty years ago," Big Joe explains. "They were holding the twentieth anniversary of the Burrito Festival—the biggest event ever to hit this town. They went all out, bringing in new rides, new attractions, and if they'd only stopped there, maybe everything would have been all right. But no, the city wanted to do something spectacular. So they introduced a brand new burrito—three-bean and broccoli."

A shudder goes through the room, as if they're all reliving the nightmare.

"This year it's going to be prune," I say.

The crowd gasps.

"Jeez, it's like they have a death wish," Tank moans.
Joe shakes his head.

"They never learn. For years, we'd been telling them that the sewers were overworked, that they needed to be expanded, modernized," he says. "But as long as we were there to keep the pipes open and fight back the mutants, they wouldn't spend a penny. So we did the best we could. We installed new toilets, reinforced the safety barriers, and put every plumber in town on high alert. And it worked for a couple of days, but on day three..."

"The restrooms on the east end went down," Tank says.

I look around the room and see a dozen nodding heads.

"We had a team there in no time, and I thought we had it under control," Joe says. "But then the west-end toilets went down. And then the north. And the south. And..."

"And that's when they came," Tank says.

Big Joe closes his eyes.

"Creatures—big ones, small ones—showed up out of nowhere. It was an invasion. They came out of the toilets, the sinks, and the gutters. Sewage was shooting out of the fountains—it looked like we'd struck oil in Mount Flushmore! If there was a pipe or a drain, they clogged it. People were panicking, screaming, running through the festival grounds. We drove the creatures back into the sewer, but then calls came from all over the city. It was the day we'd always dreaded—Plumbageddon."

"We lost three hundred toilets that day," Tiny says, gripping the counter. "They never saw what hit them."

Tank puts a hand on his shoulder.

"It took everything we had, but we won," Joe says. "And after that, we installed Merv so that it could never happen again. But it *is* happening again. And all because we can't get under that blasted dome!"

The whole place sits in a kind of stunned silence. For the first time in their lives, the great plumbers of Nitro City are helpless. Suddenly, Tiny Dinkins leaps off his barstool.

"I'll do it," he says. "I'll go into the dome."

"You?" Joe says. "You'd never even fit down the pipe. I'll do it."

"You guys wouldn't last ten seconds in the dome. I'm the one," Tank says.

The three of them stand there arguing with each

other over which of them is going to make the ultimate sacrifice, and the conversation is getting heated. Their voices are so loud that I barely hear the bell above the door, or the whispers in the crowd, or the heavy boots walking across the room.

"So," Max says. "Where's this poop chute I'm getting flushed down?"

Chapter 33

Wednesday, 1:05 p.m.

It's funny how quickly things can turn around sometimes. A few days ago, Max Bleeker was a selfish jerk,
the city was headed for a burrito-flavored doomsday,
and the Phantom Clogger was the mystery I'd never
solve. But now Max is a total hero, the Death Flush is
going to save us all, and the Phantom...

Well, let's just say he's blocked his last bowl.

I've been shadowing Scott Turbin for days, waiting
for him to make his move. And unless I miss my guess,
it's about to pay off.

I was on my way to English class when I noticed him lingering in the hall. That's not unusual by itself— but when the bell rang and Scott didn't head for a classroom, I knew he was up to something.

And I'm going to be there when it happens.

Keeping my distance, I stalk him through the building. Just as I expected—he's headed for the upstairs boys' room. Any second now, he'll look around, go through the door, and—

He passed it. He walked right by and went straight to his locker. What's he up to?

I watch him put his jacket on, then wait for him to come back my way. It's time for a little interrogation.

"Where you going, Scott?"

I say it like I already know the answer. That's how the real investigators do it.

"Leave me alone. I've got an appointment," he grunts.

"An appointment?" I say. "And where is this appointment? In the upstairs boys' room?"

Scott gives me an awkward look.

"The boys' room? Who would I have an appointment with in the boys' room?"

"Oh, I don't know," I tell him. "How about...Mr. Torpedo?"

As I say the words, I thrust forward one of the Torpedo butts I've been carrying in my pocket.

"Get that thing away from me. I don't smoke!" Scott says.

"Oh really?" I ask suspiciously, crossing my arms.

"Yeah, really. I can't be near a cigarette. I've got asthma."

"Asthma?"

"Yeah. That's where I'm going right now, to get my breathing treatment. I've got an appointment every Wednesday afternoon. I thought everybody knew that."

Hmmmm...Now that he mentions it, it does sound familiar. And if Scott is telling the truth—and there's a first time for everything—he couldn't be the Clogger. Because unless I've got my dates mixed up, at least two of the attacks happened on Wednesday afternoons.

"Now get out of my way. My mom's waiting."

I step aside to let him pass, but there's still one more question I need answered.

"Scott," I say, "did you put that toilet seat in my desk?"

"I wish," he tells me, a baboon-like grin on his face. "That was genius!"

"Yeah," I say. "It was."

That's my problem. It was way too smart for Scott to pull off, and light-years ahead of Mumford.

I let Scott pass because he's got to go to a doctor's appointment, and I've got to go back to square one.

Leonard is going to have a fit.

I decide to make a pit stop before I go back to English class. The upstairs boys' room is handy, so I pop inside.

"Well, well, well," Mumford Milligan says, and he takes a long drag off his cigarette. "If it isn't the Toilet King."

He's not alone. Skeeter Harper is here, too. Skeeter's not as big as Mumford, but with his blue spiked mohawk and small yellow teeth, he looks just as scary.

"Hey guys," I say, trying to sound friendly. "What's that you're smoking there, Skeeter? Is that a Torpedo?"

"Torpedo?" he says, giving me a twisted sneer. "What am I, eighty? Torpedoes are an old man's cigarette."

"Yeah, don't you know anything?" Mumford says. "The only one in this school who smokes Torpedoes is Mr. Krumsky."

Mr. Krumsky? Of course! The janitor. He comes in early, he's got access to every restroom, and there are tons of clogging supplies right in his office. Why didn't I think of it before? The Phantom is Mr. Krumsky!

"Excuse me," I say. "I just thought of something I need to do."

But before I can reach the door, Skeeter steps in front of it. His yellow teeth look like menacing little butter pats.

"Hope you brought your trunks," he hisses. "Because you're going swimming."

I'd like to answer, to say something clever, brave, and devastating, but I can't because there's a lump the size of an eight ball in my throat. In Gloomy Valley, going swimming means just one thing: the swimming hole.

Around here, the swimming hole is the popular name for stall number three—the toilet that never comes clean. Mumford grabs one of my arms, and Skeeter gets the other. The two of them drag me across the floor and through the creaky metal door.

"Hold your breath," Mumford says, pushing my head toward the terrible bowl.

After all my years of being around toilets, you'd

think swirlies wouldn't really bother me. But they do. I hate them, probably because I've seen too much. I arch my back and try to keep my head up, but it only makes him push harder. The porcelain torture device is getting closer, and closer, and—

REEEEEEEEEEEEEK!

The creature's shriek is high-pitched and earsplitting! The three of us spring backward like we were loaded in the same slingshot.

My face has barely cleared the rim when an oozing, unearthly blob explodes out of the toilet. Mumford and Skeeter, looking terrified, let go and tumble over each other as they escape from the stall. I'm not so lucky. I fall to the floor, and when I look up, I find myself staring at a horrible, wormlike beast with a mouth as big as my head.

It's a gargantuan super-slug.

The super-slug is basically a big squishy glob of awful with wriggling tentacles and a bad attitude. I kick the creature in its enormous gut and throw myself against the stall door. The slug quickly disappears back down the toilet hole, and a second later, I hear its terrible shriek again...only this time, it's coming from stall number one.

I race to the other stall and throw open the door just in time to see the creature disappear again. The one thing I know about super-slugs is that as long as there's an open toilet, they're going to keep finding a way out.

And there are toilets all over the school.

I wait for it to appear again, but when it doesn't, I head downstairs. As soon as I'm inside the restroom, I hear a noise in the second stall. Suddenly, the metal door bursts open.

"Nixon? What are you doing in here?"

He squints his gopher eyes.

"None of your beeswax, nosy. Can't a guy even—"

"Nixon!" I scream.

But it's too late. The slug bursts from the bowl behind him, and before he even knows what's happening, it slurps him down like a milk shake through a straw. I lunge for him but only manage to grab his sneaker. It comes off in my hand.

He's gone. Nixon is gone!

I want to scream, but I can't. The air's been ripped from my lungs, pushed out by the real-life horror movie I just saw. My best friend—eaten alive right in front of my eyes!

The super-slug slithers across the tile floor, and I jump back against the wall. I lift my foot, ready to stomp on its neck, only it doesn't come after me. Actually, it doesn't do much of anything. It just sort of lies there, tentacles flopping around like weeds in the wind. I think it's sick.

Really sick. I hear a weird gurgling noise, then a sound like a malfunctioning tuba. A second later, the creature gasps, flattens out, and—

GLOOOOOOP!

A disgusting stream of slime shoots out the tail end of the squishy body. In the middle of it is Nixon.

Well, Nixon and a bunch of slug poo.

"You're alive!"

He goes into a coughing fit and spits out what I can only assume is a lungful of intestines. I kneel down beside him.

"You okay?" I ask.

He gasps in a huge breath of air, then grabs me by my collar.

"We never speak of this to *anyone!*" he says.

I nod and help him to his feet. Meanwhile, the creature starts slowly crawling back toward the bowl. I rush for it, but it vanishes into the drain before I get there.

"We need to hurry," I tell Nixon. "We've got to block every bowl hole in the building."

"Block them with what?" he says.

"Come with me."

We run to the janitor's office, but there's no sign of Mr. Krumsky. The door is open, so we walk inside.

"Grab that box," I say.

He picks up a small brown box with a dozen spray cans inside.

"Bug bombs?" he says.

Bug bombs, or roach foggers, or whatever you want to call them, are canisters of vaporized insect-doom that spray a gaseous, poisonous mist into the atmosphere. It's a little trick I learned from Max. The tall, skinny cans are the perfect size to block a toilet drain, and the toxic spray repels even the stubbornest super-slug.

"You take the downstairs bathrooms, I'll take the upstairs," I say. "Activate the spray nozzle and then stuff the can into the toilet as far as it'll go. Make sure you block the opening tight."

"Got it," he says.

We race through the building, stopping up toilets with our poisonous canned clogs. The good news is, there's no sign of the monster. I guess slurping down one chubby eighth-grader was more than it could handle.

I meet Nixon on the stairs.

"All done?"

He nods, and we collapse on the steps. Whew! That could've been a disaster. But except for Nixon taking a joyride through a mutant's colon, I think we did pretty well. He got the boys' and girls' bathrooms downstairs, I got the boys' and girls' bathrooms upstairs. And even as we sit here, the school's pipes and drains are filling up with toxic vapor. We're covered.

"Is that spray stuff safe?" Nixon says.

"Yeah. It's supposed to be flammable, but we're fine as long as nobody tries to flush an open flame. Can you imagine? If they did, the whole thing might go off like a—"

Oh no.

"Torpedo!" I gasp.

The faculty bathroom! We forgot the faculty bathroom! I rush up the stairs. There's a royal-blue cleaning cart parked outside the faculty's tiny single-serve restroom.

"Mr. Krumsky!" I yell. "Whatever you do, don't flush your cig—"

KA-BOOOOOOM!

Several gut-wrenching seconds pass, and then the restroom door opens. A thick cloud of black smoke pours into the hall, and out of it walks Mr. Krumsky. He looks like the burned side of a toasted marshmallow. I peek into the bathroom. There's a large hole in the ceiling that leads all the way to the sky.

What happened to the toilet that made it, I have no idea.

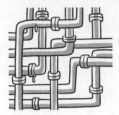

Chapter 34

Thursday, 6:14 p.m.

"You blew up the school?"

If a phone call from your mother starts this way, chances are the rest of it isn't going to be good.

"I didn't blow up the school. Just a bathroom…and a janitor. But it wasn't my fault."

On the screen, my mother's face looks madder than I ever thought a face could look. My dad is right next to her, but he just looks scared.

"What was the last thing I told you when we left?" Mom says. "I said, 'Don't cause any trouble.' And what

I meant was 'don't play your music too loud' or 'don't break a window with a baseball,' because I never even imagined you'd pull something like this!"

"Look, I can explain everything. You see—"

"Don't bother, your principal already filled me in. And I also had the pleasure of seeing your name in the newspaper!" she says.

It's funny how parents are always happy to see your name in the paper as long as it's because you won the spelling bee or made a touchdown. But get in there for sending a toilet into orbit, and it's like it's the end of the world.

"I'm sorry, Sully. We've had a family discussion, and we all agree that we need to make a change," Mom says.

My dad leans backward until he's out of my mom's view. Then he stealthily shakes his head and points to her, letting me know he was not part of this decision.

Mom rolls her eyes.

"Phil, I can see you in the little window on the monitor," she says.

Dad slumps over and hugs his knees.

"Sully, your principal thinks you should finish out the semester, but that's it. I've already talked to Big

Joe, and he's making arrangements to get you to your new school."

"Basher Academy? But that's not—"

"Fair?" Mom interrupts me. "I'll tell you what's not fair. It's not fair when a mother has to move halfway around the world and leave her son without proper supervision. But I did it because I trusted you, and I thought it was better than the alternative. I've been more than fair, and we see how that worked out. Now I'm going to be smart."

There's some more discussion, a lot of it loud, but the bottom line is this: a toilet exploded in Nitro City and blew me all the way to the meanest military school in the state. That has to be some kind of a record.

Chapter 35

Friday, 9:12 p.m.

Standing in the shadow of the super-toilet, Tank Huberman addresses the troops.

"You're all plumbers, so I don't have to tell you about leaks. A leak is our enemy, a disaster waiting to happen. You never know what one little drip might turn into. That's why this mission has to remain absolutely secret. Not a word to anyone. So if you don't think you can keep your mouth shut," he says, holding up a roll of duct tape, "I've got something to seal it right here. Everybody got that?"

All around me, plumbers are nodding like bobble-head dolls.

"Good. Now let's get to work!"

Tank has a knack for getting people's attention. But not everyone is listening. Big Joe and Max are off in the corner going over some last-minute details.

"Max? Max?" Big Joe says.

Max is drinking a soda and bouncing a tennis ball off the wall. He doesn't respond.

"Pay attention, man. Everything depends on you."

"Relax, I've got it," Max says, chugging the soda and crushing the can. "Get flushed, find Marv, don't die. Piece of cake."

"Marv?" Joe says, worry lines popping out of his forehead. "You mean Merv."

"Whatever."

He gives the ball another bounce. Joe holds up a long chain with a key on the end.

"Now when you find the valve, you use this."

"Turn the key, open the valve, save the day. Got it," Max says.

He sounds like a bored parrot just waiting on the cracker. Tiny and Tank wander over and stand next to me.

"All right," Joe says. "Well, I think that covers it. Do you have any questions?"

"Just one," says Max, snagging the tennis ball in mid-flight. "How do I get out?"

The question sits there untouched, like a sneezed-on cupcake.

"Well, uh..." Joe says.

Max starts bouncing the ball again.

"Yeah. That's what I thought."

It's a cruel moment—crueler than an empty birthday piñata.

"Don't worry, Max," Tiny says. "You'll be all right. The sewer angels always watch over us plumbers."

Ever since I was old enough to hold a pipe wrench, I've heard stories about the sewer angels—underground guardians who look down from above.

"Oh, here we go again," Tank mumbles.

"Just because you can't see them doesn't mean they're not there," Tiny says.

But Max isn't paying attention. He's just standing there with his super-hair and sunglasses, bouncing the yellow ball over, and over, and over.

Big Joe moves beside him.

"Look, son," he says, "I'm not going to lie to you,

the odds are slim. But if anyone can fight their way through and make it out again, it's you. I believe that, Max. You're what we call an Unflushable. And the thing about Unflushables is you can't keep 'em down. They always rise to the top."

Max stops bouncing the ball and puts it in his pocket. Without saying another word, he walks out the door.

I feel kind of sick to my stomach. To be honest, it never even occurred to me that Max might not make it out of there. I mean, if he's said it once, he's said it a thousand times: *"Dying is for losers."*

"All right," the Moleman yells from the toilet rim. "Everybody out of the pool!"

Plumbers emerge from everywhere. They come from out of the bowl, underneath the floor, and the space above the ceiling. They're grabbing tools, ladders, and ropes, and hurrying away from the flush zone.

"What's happening?" I ask.

"It's ready," Joe says.

The Moleman moves across the room and stops in front of a large control panel. He flips a switch and presses a few buttons. It lights up like a Christmas tree.

"Well, here goes," he says. "Activating!"

He presses the red button in the center of the panel. My heart picks up speed. I hear a low rumble, then a loud whirring noise like a jet engine starting up. The next few seconds seem to take forever, but then streams of water burst out of the pipes! They flow into the giant toilet like sparkling-clean rivers filling the ocean.

The only thing more beautiful than that great porcelain waterfall is the sight taking place all around me. Dozens of old plumbers are cheering, laughing, and dancing. Tank and Tiny are hugging each other and spinning in a circle. And Big Joe—well, he's just soaking it up like a dream he doesn't want to forget.

"I'm going to go check on Max," I say.

When I get outside, Max is nowhere in sight, which is fine with me. What was I going to say? Sorry I talked you into getting death-flushed? Have a nice trip? No, the best thing anybody can do for Max is leave him alone.

Max isn't the reason I came out here. I came out here to do something I've been dreading for days.

I pull out my phone, hit video chat, and dial. A few seconds later, April Danvers's blue eyes are looking back at me.

"It's you!" she says, her face breaking into a smile.

"Hi, April. Look, there's something I've got to—"

"Oh, hold on!" she says, and puts down her phone. When she returns, there's a pink hatula on her head.

"Look what came in the mail."

I roll my eyes.

"I am so sorry."

"Why? I love it. I'm going to wear it to the festival tomorrow."

The lump in my throat feels like it's made out of lead.

"I can't go to the Burrito Festival with you, April," I tell her.

"Oh," she says.

Her expression is cute and sad at the same time, like an unsold puppy in a pet shop window.

"Yeah. Something's come up."

It's not the greatest excuse, but it's the only one I've got.

"Okay," she says, sounding disappointed. "I guess I'll just go by myself."

"No!" I tell her, louder than I intended. "You shouldn't go to the festival at all. Look, I can't explain, but it's not safe—not this year."

"What are you talking about?"

"All I can tell you is that there's this group that thinks something bad is going to happen, and they've got a plan to stop it. I'm here working on it right now."

"You're there now?"

"Yeah, and I need to get back inside. But I had to warn you. And you can't tell anybody."

"But—"

"*Nobody*. If I could explain, I—"

"What are you doing?"

It's Max's voice. He's standing right behind me.

"I've got to go, April. I'll talk to you later."

I click off. Max gives me a long, uncomfortable look.

"What? I had to make a phone call," I say.

The stare doesn't ease up.

"Guess you better get back in there," he says at last.

I shove the phone in my pocket and head into the warehouse. The group is gathered in a huddle, and there's a loud argument going on.

"Look, I'm going, and that's all there is to it," Big Joe says. "Someone's gotta get onto the festival grounds. We have to be able to monitor the situation. And if something happens, maybe I can hold off the worst of it until Bleeker gets through."

"By yourself? That's crazy, Joe!" Tank yells. "Anyway, you'll never get in. The Icks will be on you before you reach the gate. It's impossible!"

"I know it's impossible! But what choice do we have? It's the only way," Joe says.

A hush falls over the room, and the only sound is water filling the gigantic bowl. A tall, lanky figure looks down from the ladder leading to the rim.

"Oh, what to do, what to do?" the Moleman says, wiping little pretend-tears out of his eyes. "How will you ever manage to breach something as impenetrable as a city park entrance? Why, that would take some kind of evil genius! If only there was one around who could come up with a plan..."

Chapter 36

Saturday, 11:02 a.m.

"I can't believe you're really doing this," I say.

"Believe it," Joe tells me.

"There must be another way. No offense, but do you have to wear that ridiculous costume? People are staring at us."

"If it embarrasses you, go home."

"I just hope nobody from school sees me," I say. "If we run into anyone I know, pretend we're not together."

I hope Joe is nodding, but there's really no way to tell. Not when he's in that stupid suit. I don't mean the Flush—I'd be honored to stand with the Midnight Flush. No, I mean the one he's wearing right now... Beanie the Burrito.

That's right, I'm walking around the festival in full public view with a humongous talking burrito. Being the Toilet King is nothing compared to this.

"Couldn't the Moleman have come up with something less humiliating?"

"You know a better way to blend in?" Joe says.

He's got me there. Beanie the Burrito is the festival's official mascot. He's a human-sized foam-rubber burrito with pinto beans for feet and shredded cheese for hair. There are probably a dozen Beanies walking around here, and a lot of other costumed characters, too. So as much as I hate to admit it, this really is the perfect disguise.

Me? I'm just in dark sunglasses and the hatula that my mom sent me. I suppose if someone really looked close, they could tell who I am, but when you've got a big spatula sticking out of your forehead, people tend not to make eye contact.

I look down the aisles and drool a little. I mean, the Burrito Festival is always fun, but for the fiftieth anniversary, they've gone all out. There are twice as many booths as last year, and a lot more rides. How am I supposed to be on patrol when all I can think about is the Flyin' Burrito Mean Bean Plungin' Machine? It's a roller coaster where you're strapped into a burrito-shaped cart that takes you along a twisting, winding track before passing through a humongous mouth full of giant motorized teeth. Then it's a 120-mile-per-hour face-plunge down a long, steep esophagus that splashes into a vat of stomach acid.

It's not real stomach acid, it's just smelly, green water. But it sort of burns like stomach acid, so at least that's something.

We make our way across the park and stop in front of Mount Flushmore. It's the heart of the entire festival, a massive stone sculpture of a toilet surrounded by four of history's greatest plumbers: Wild Bill Sullivan, Plungerella, Kip "The Drip" Kiper, and Captain Clog.

Everywhere I look, I see blue work shirts. Ick-y blue.

A hand grabs my shoulder.

"Max? What are you doing here? Aren't you supposed to be at—"

"Relax, I'm just getting the lay of the land," he says. "Might as well, there's nothing I can do back at the Moleman's place. Apparently, he's still got to test the thing, make sure it's safe enough to death-flush me. And after it flushes, it won't be ready again for twenty-four hours."

He turns to Big Joe.

"Big crowd. What do you think?"

"Looks normal enough. But it's just the first day," Joe says. "The system hasn't had time to overload. My money's on day three, just like the last time. So for now, just stroll around, keep your eyes open, and pretend you're having fun."

"I'm hanging out with Beanie the Burrito and Spatula-head," Max says. "Who needs to pretend?"

We walk to the far side of the park, then start back again. The prune burritos seem to be big sellers, but other than that, I haven't noticed anything strange.

A loudspeaker on a utility pole makes a high-pitched squeal.

"Attention, visitors, the restrooms on the west side of the midway are currently out of order. We apologize for the inconvenience."

I look at Joe.

"Let's go," he says.

The midway is my favorite part of the festival. It's where you find the best rides, games, and booths. Well, it's where most people find them. Me? I'm checking out the restroom.

The closed restroom.

There's nothing especially unusual about it. It's just a long brick building blocked off with some orange cones, and an OUT OF ORDER sign. Two bored-looking Icks are out front, turning people away.

"Seems okay from down here," I say. "Maybe we should have a look from the roller coaster."

Big Joe gives me a googly-eyed stare.

"It might be nothing, just an opening-day glitch," he says. "It's hard to tell."

"I can probably sneak inside," Max says, but Joe shakes his head.

"No, we can't risk—"

Suddenly, there's a scream. It came from the restroom on the other side of the aisle. When I turn around, I see a terrified woman run out of the building just as a group of Icks rushes in.

They don't stay long. A nasty-looking croctopus follows them out the door. A few seconds later, two enormous sewer rats burst out of the gutter.

The midway erupts in panic.

Joe peels off the bulky foam burrito costume.

Underneath it, he's decked out in his famous silver coveralls and black mask.

"It's the Midnight Flush!" someone yells. "The Flush is here!"

The crowd moves in around us, and so do some Icks, but Joe pays no attention. He straps on a headset and speaks into a tiny microphone.

"I need everybody on the midway now!"

By "everybody," he means, well, everybody. Everybody from the Poo, anyway. I watch as an army of costumed characters races through the festival aisles. Running our way are giant burritos, tomatoes, avocados, peppers, chickens, cows, and a supersized soda cup. As the costumes are torn away, I see, for the first time in my life, the fully outfitted heroes of P.L.U.N.G.E.

From the north end comes Maximum Flo, Tiny Dinkins, and Under Woman. From the south, I see Water Warrior, Commander Two-Ply, Long John Plunger, and the Unstoppable Drain. Finally, from the west, moving like a runaway freight train, is the Tank.

More plumbers come, too, but Max doesn't notice. His eyes have never left the croc.

"I'm going in," he says.

"No!" Joe yells. "You've got to get to the Moleman.

Sully, go with him, and stop that test. We can't wait another twenty-four hours. It's got to be now. We'll handle things here."

Max doesn't budge. I've seen him lock his sights on a creature before; he doesn't like walking away from a fight.

"Come on!" I yell, throwing my weight against his body.

Finally, he gives in, and we move toward the front gate. We're nearly there when a small mob of blue work shirts—seven, maybe eight of them—blocks our path. I recognize the one in front. It's the bushy-haired Ick from the black SUV. He's missing his two front teeth.

"Going somewhere, Max?" he asks.

The words come out with a whistling sound.

Max calmly takes out his phone, and holds it to his ear.

"Plan B," he says.

That's all. And then he hangs up.

"What's plan B?" I ask.

"Just get to the Moleman," he tells me.

A grin crosses his face just before he charges into the pack. He bashes one with his elbow and punches another in the jaw. There's a massive struggle as they close in around him. I see a heavy black flashlight rise into the air, then come down hard across Max's neck. He goes to his knees. When he looks up at me, there's anger in his eyes.

"Go!" he yells.

I break into a dead run. As I near the front gate, I can still hear the fists pounding like hammers. Blazing past a restroom station, I'm barely aware of someone screaming, and then I see a shadow quickly growing over me.

CRAAA-AAASH!

A flying urinal lands two feet away.

I sidestep it and never look back.

Chapter 37

Saturday, 2:37 p.m.

The subway station is two blocks away. I jump on the train and count each agonizing second until we reach my stop. This would be so much simpler if I could just call the Moleman. But if he has a phone, I've never seen it. Even Izzy couldn't get in touch with him.

When the train stops, I leap through the door and start running. I just hope it's not already too late.

I sprint several blocks until I see the warehouse. It's just ahead. I'm almost to the door when a dark blur streaks past me and slides to a stop in front of the building. It's a motorcycle. A motorcycle with a rider dressed in black.

She takes off her helmet. My mouth opens like a sinkhole.

"You're...you're..."

"Plan B," One-Eyed Lily Cruz says.

She slides back the heavy steel door and walks inside. I follow along, too starstruck to speak.

When we reach the back area, the Moleman is darting around the room, twisting knobs and setting dials.

"Well, Sullivan, how nice of you join us," he says, tapping his finger against a temperature gauge. "And look, you brought a friend."

"Hello, Moleman," Lily says.

"Hello, Lily. How is my favorite S.S.S. agent?"

"S.S.S.?" I blurt out. "You're with the Secret Sewer Service?"

She winks at me. Or maybe she's blinking—it's kind of hard to tell with the eye patch. All of a sudden, I'm keenly aware that I'm standing next to an enormous white toilet, and I remember why I'm here.

"Don't flush it!" I scream.

"Wow," Izzy says. "There's a sentence you don't hear every day."

Izzy. I should've known she'd be here. Why does my archnemesis want to horn in on everything I do?

"Calm down, Sullivan. We canceled the test," the Moleman says.

"Yeah, we saw what's happening at the Burrito Festival," Izzy says. "It's all over the news."

She picks up the remote control and points it at a TV in the corner. Channel 6 news anchor Pepper Hayes is talking.

"We're getting numerous reports of absolute chaos at the Burrito Festival," she says, smiling warmly at the camera. "Officials say the plumbing system has completely failed, and that the grounds are being overrun by mutants. Ironwater chairman Herman Wiest has released a statement saying the system was sabotaged by the rebel organization P.L.U.N.G.E., and that the Midnight Flush was spotted at the scene. The situation is deteriorating, and residents are advised to stay in their homes. On a lighter note, what's the weather going to be like for day two of the festival, Doppler Doug?"

Izzy turns off the TV.

"It sounds like your friends have their hands full," the Moleman says, flipping a row of red switches. "If I

239

get the chance, I'll send over a few of my more inter-esting devices. You know what they say: you can never have too many superweapons. Of course, not all of them have been tested yet…oh, well, what's the worst that can happen? I maim a few plumbers—I used to do that for a living."

"He's been running around like crazy getting every-thing ready," Izzy says.

"And it's ready right now," he tells us. "Where is my flush-tronaut?"

I think back to the sight of Max being mobbed by the Icks. My stomach starts doing somersaults.

"Change of plans," Lily says. "I'm going instead."

"You?" the Moleman says. "Do you know what you're doing?"

"I'm opening a valve. Max said I'll know it when I see it."

He shrugs.

"A flush is a flush, I suppose. All right, when I push this red button, you start up the ladder, and—"

I hear the warehouse door open.

"Hello?" I yell. "Hello?"

"Hello, partner," Cowboy answers. "Long time no see."

He's standing there with a smug, sickening grin on his face, his shaved head glistening like a new bowling ball. Lily starts toward him, but he waves his hand.

"Not this time, little lady," he says.

Twenty blue-shirted goons march into the room. They're carrying long metal poles that look like electric cattle prods. Cowboy steps forward and stares at the Death Flush.

"I gotta hand it to you. That is one king-sized crapper. Just what were you planning on doing with that thing?"

"Flushing waste," the Moleman says. "Hop in."

Cowboy's grin turns into a smile.

"I like you, old-timer, you make me laugh. Now why don't you go ahead and shut this contraption down?"

"It's a lengthy process," the Moleman says.

"Then you best get started," Cowboy tells him.

The Moleman walks to the back wall. Cowboy sends half the Icks out to the front of the warehouse to watch for incoming plumbers. Then he points to three chairs and tells Lily, Izzy, and me to sit down. When I do, he puts a hand on my shoulder and squeezes.

"I hear you're planning something. Something big," he says, then glances up at the toilet. "Real big."

"Where'd you hear that?" I say.

I see the wall of Icks part, and a slim, yellow-haired girl steps through the gap.

"He heard it from me."

If my jaw wasn't attached to my skull, it would be on the floor right now.

"April? How did you get here?"

"I brought her," Cowboy says. "I kind of had to. It's Bring Your Daughter to Work Day."

Daughter? Did he just say "daughter"?

April walks toward me.

"Actually, it isn't Bring Your Daughter to Work Day," she says. "I just told my dad that so I could come along. And he believed me. But people always believe me, don't they, Sully?"

She smiles at me, and for the first time I can see that the little sparkle in her blue eyes isn't a sparkle at all. It's evil. Concentrated evil.

Cowboy shakes his head.

"Don't feel too bad, kid," he says. "My daughter can manipulate anybody. She's like an artist. That's why we sent her to find you."

"Me?" I say.

He waves a finger at me.

"You were the great Gloomy Valley mystery. See, we had plumbing systems breaking down at every school in the city, but for some reason, Gloomy Valley never needed a repair. Not so much as a leaky faucet. That seemed odd to us. So I sent in April to find out why. You see—"

I finish his sentence for him. "The best way to find out if someone is secretly fixing toilets is to have someone secretly break them," I say. "Your daughter's the Phantom Clogger."

April gives me a slow handclap.

"Bravo, you solved the case," she says. "I was starting to think you'd never figure it out. There was a little while there when I worried you were getting close, and that's when I framed Scott. It was easy. I put the toilet seat in your chair, sprayed Heartthrob cologne in the bathroom, and planted a few cigarette butts in his locker."

"And Mr. Krumsky?" I say.

"Pure luck," she says. "He's been flushing his Torpedoes for years. That's why you found them at every clog—they were stuck there in the filter and spilled out when the toilet backed up. But you just knew they were some kind of master clue, little pieces of evidence intentionally left behind as a signature. Naturally, I didn't have the heart to correct you."

I almost bite through my lip. No one should be this good at being bad.

"One thing I still don't understand," I say. "How did you know about this place?"

"Oh, I almost forgot the best part!" she says, and there's terrible glee in her voice. "Remember when you called me to break the horrible news that you couldn't go to the Burrito Festival? It was awfully thoughtful of you to do it in a video chat. That's how I got this."

She lifts her phone and shows me a screenshot. It's a picture of me standing in front of the warehouse. An address—111 Tesla Street—is painted on the wall. But that's not the only thing the picture shows. It shows who's standing behind me.

"That's how you knew about Max!" I explode.

"I never could have done it without you," she says.

She's right, she couldn't. This is all my fault. Everything.

"You're a monster," I tell her.

April stares at me, and for the first time, her blue eyes look like ice.

"You've seen what's happening at the Burrito Festival,

Sully. Let me tell you how it ends," she says, and moves in close to whisper in my ear. "The monsters win."

The Moleman finishes whatever he's doing at the back wall and moves to the control panel.

"Ah, yes, this should do it," he says, and there's a clicking sound as he types something on a keyboard.

Suddenly a metal door closes, separating this room from the front of the warehouse. I hear the Icks pounding on it from the outside. The Moleman presses a button, and jets of steam release into the room, creating a thick, blinding fog.

Cowboy leaps at the Moleman, and the two of them wrestle on the floor.

Like a rocket, Lily blasts out of her chair, hitting one Ick with a side kick, and another with a back-fist. She moves through the room, barely touching the ground as she goes on the attack. I hear deep, painful groans as her boot flies from blue shirt to blue shirt. The Icks chase her to the far side of the room.

Which means I've got one chance.

I run to the control panel and hit the red button. Next to it, I see a key on a cord—the same key Big Joe showed Max. I grab it, put the cord around my neck, and head for the ladder.

But I don't make it. April is standing in the way, holding one of the stun-sticks. When she hits the trigger, a spark shoots across the tip, and she pokes it at me like a spear.

"You're not going anywhere."

I see something moving in the fog, and then a fist connects with April's jaw—Izzy's fist. April goes down, and Izzy flings herself on top of her.

"Whoa," I say. "Izzy, I didn't know you could—"

"Just shut up and get in the toilet!" she yells.

The next thing I know, I'm standing on the rim of the Death Flush.

And I jump.

Chapter 38

Saturday, 3:50 p.m.

The best way to describe getting death-flushed is that it's like a waterslide, but with more butt-burn and practically no chance of survival. You'd think this would make it less fun, and you'd be right. I am twisting down a long, sloping pipe that's just barely wide enough for my body. I've got no idea how fast I'm going, I only know that it's scary— but not nearly as scary as that noise up ahead. What is that, anyway? It sounds like an angry giant slamming the trunk of his car.

When I peek between my feet, I catch a glimpse

of what's waiting for me. Two heavy doors lined with sharp metal teeth are opening and closing like the jaws of an alligator. They smash together, crushing anything that comes between them. I slide closer. The doors collide, and this time I have to curl my toes just to avoid a pedicure. Before the teeth can take another bite, my body rockets into the gap, and I'm staring directly into the bone cruncher above me. And then—*SMACK!*

I get the most uncomfortable haircut of my life.

Suddenly, the pipe makes a steep, downward plunge, and I pick up speed. The result is the dreaded super-wedgie, the kind you have to remove with tweezers.

I'll say this much for Ironwater—when they put in security features, they go all out.

SCHEEEEING!

What was that?

SCHEEEEING!

A metal spike slashes by my face!

SCHEEEEING!

Then by my leg…

SCHEEEEING!

…and under my arm…

SCHEEEEING!

…and across my belly. They're shooting out all

around me, and I feel like I'm in the middle of a homicidal pincushion. Each skewer misses me by inches, and just when I think this long, horror-filled ride will never end—it does.

Well, the pipe ends, anyway.

I'm midair, launched into open space, streaking through sky-high nothingness, about to face an old enemy...

Gravity.

I drop like a screaming cannonball. After what feels like an eternity, I land on something soft and squishy.

Ewwwwww. I don't know what broke my fall, but it's thick, wet, and smells like the bus station. Don't get me wrong, I'm glad I'm alive, but now I'm trapped in quicksand's ugly cousin, and the more I struggle, the faster I sink. My only choice is to tunnel my way out. It's like digging through a mountain of pudding, except not awesome.

After a lot of extreme gagging, I break out of the squishy prison. Exhausted, I roll onto my back and wait for my head to clear. It does, and what I see is terrifying and glorious—and huge.

The dome!

I made it. I'm inside the Nitrodome. It stretches out

in all directions like an endless steel sky. For plumbers, this is like finding Atlantis. I don't know exactly what goes on in here, but it sure doesn't look like the rest of the sewer. For one thing, I'm in an enormous room as tall as a skyscraper. I can see something like a mountain in the distance, only it's covered in little dots. The area around me looks like a jungle, but there's something strange about it. I climb to my feet and look closer, and now I see what it is—these aren't trees. They're mushrooms. Gigantic mutant mushrooms with trunks like redwoods and caps that tower over my head.

How am I supposed to find some stupid valve in a place like this? I don't even know where to start.

Out of the corner of my eye, I see something that looks like a fly crawling across a wall. Only it isn't a fly. I squint hard and try to squeeze out a better view, but it's pretty far away. What is that? Is that what I think it is? No, it can't be. It can't be...but it is.

It's a truck.

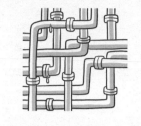

Chapter 39

Saturday, 4:24 p.m.

It's hot, and even though I haven't been walking that long, it's starting to get to me. I'm so thirsty I could drink toilet water. Blue toilet water. Maybe that's it—maybe I'm delirious. I mean, how can there be a truck in a place with no way in and no way out? It's impossible.

Then again, I'm here. That's supposed to be impossible, too.

I move through the mega-mushrooms, pushing through thick, moldy strands of slime that feel even grosser than they look. But what really bothers me is what I hear. It's a freaky sound, somewhere between a grunt and a growl.

What is that?

It's probably just my stomach. Stomachs make all sorts of weird noises, right? On Taco Tuesday, our school cafeteria sounds like a room full of angry cats playing the bassoon. So that sound could be anything. Or nothing.

But it isn't nothing. It's something, and it's standing about ten feet in front of me, snarling, teeth bared, and looking at me like I'm a gigantic carrot. Which wouldn't be especially terrifying if this were a croctopus or an apocalypse cow, but it's not.

It's a bunny.

Only not the cuddly kind of bunny. This thing is the size of a moose, with gigantic claws and two long fangs jutting out from under its twitching pink nose. And it's coming this way.

I dart into the fungus forest, and the creature is right behind me. All that bulk has cost it some speed, but not as much as you'd think. I glance over my shoulder just as the creature makes its leap. At the last instant, I do a sharp right turn and tuck roll out of the way. The rabbit sails over me, almost like it's flying, and then—it stops.

I can't believe what I'm seeing. It's like I'm watching a movie put on pause. Because this enormous, raging hare of hate is just hanging there, frozen in midflight like a kite caught in a tree. I hear a sound like raindrops tapping on the tops of the mushrooms, and when I look up, I spot what appears to be a huge black cloud passing overhead.

Only this is no cloud.

Directly above me, so close I can see the drool on its mandibles, is a massive, black, nightmare-inducing spider. I duck as low as I can, but it doesn't seem to matter. It's not here for me.

The eight legs of death crawl across the mushroom caps, then slink down the invisible web toward the big, fluffy monster. The captured rabbit bares its fangs.

I don't know how the battle between them is going to turn out, and I'm not waiting around to see. Because something a little more interesting just grabbed my attention. Remember that mountain I saw in the distance? The one with the dots? Well, it's a lot closer now, and I'm getting my first good look at it.

Turns out it's actually a huge structure carved directly

into the underground walls. And those dots? They're tunnels. It's riddled with them. Maybe I'm wrong, but my gut tells me one of them will lead me to Merv.

Moving quickly, I make my way across the clearing and enter the first tunnel I come to. I should probably ease my way through it, make sure there are no surprises, but I haven't got time. Big Joe and the others are counting on me. I wonder how they're holding up. Or how many of them might already be—

No. I push the thought out of my head.

I follow the tunnel until it connects with a maze of dark, skinny roads that run in every direction. Which way next? I don't know. I'm turned around, and they all look pretty much the same. I'm about to choose one at random when I hear voices.

That's the last thing I ever expected to hear under the Nitrodome. I move toward them.

There it is—the truck I saw. It looks like one of those military vehicles, the kind with a cab in the front and a large cargo bed covered by a green canvas top. Two men are standing beside it and talking. I hide in the shadows and wait.

"We're supposed to dump all this?" a man in gray coveralls asks.

His partner shrugs.

"That's what they said—dump the whole load here. Just don't get any on you. I hear this stuff'll make you grow tentacles."

The men are pouring heavy-looking barrels into a metal grate on the sewer floor. A greenish liquid spills out. Some of it splashes to the side and forms a small, smelly river that just misses my feet. When they're finished, they load the barrels on the truck and get back in the cab.

As quietly as I can, I move in closer and look into the metal grate. It's dark down there, but I see something big and slimy slither by. Whatever it is, it gives me the creeps. Suddenly, the truck starts to pull away. I catch hold of the tailgate and pull myself inside, then hide behind one of barrels. That's when I see the name printed on it.

MUTA-NIX, it says.

Muta-Nix? Muta-Nix is the stuff Ironwater makes people flush down their toilets to keep mutants away. At least that's what they say in their commercials.

I scrunch myself into the corner, trying very hard not to get any on me.

After a short drive, we stop. I hear something that

sounds like a gate opening, and then we're moving again. When I peek out the back, I see that we're in a parking garage filled with trucks that look just like this one. Lots of trucks.

What is going on down here?

The doors open, and when the men leave, I climb out of the back. As I make my way through the garage, I check out the other vehicles. Some are empty, some have boxes—this one looks like it's carrying a load of laundry. Dirty laundry, but I can't afford to be picky. I reach into the back and grab the first thing I can get my hands on, which turns out to be a long white lab coat. I slip it on. It fits me about as well as my dad's bathrobe, but it's better than looking like I just fell out of a sewer pipe.

Anyway, there's no time to shop around. A group of people in the same gray coveralls are headed my way. I start moving again, trying to stay ahead of them, but they're still coming, and I'm running out of garage. A few more steps and I'll be cornered.

Behind me, there's a sudden rumble, like quiet thunder, and I nearly jump out of my skin. When I turn around, two heavy steel doors open next to me. I rush inside.

"Hey, hold the elevator!" someone yells.

Frantically, I push the Up button.

"I said hold the elevator!"

The footsteps are getting closer, and I hear the sound of running. I hold my breath. Finally, the doors start to close.

"Hey!" the man yells, and his hand makes a desperate reach for the door.

But he's too late. The shiny steel barriers close just in time, and I'm on my way up.

Up to where, I have no idea.

Chapter 40

Saturday, 5:52 p.m.

DING!

The metal doors slide open again. I stick my head outside and look around. Nobody in sight, just a long, curved hallway with charcoal-gray carpet and beige walls. It reminds me of the airport. I step out of the elevator and ease my way down the hall.

"Can I help you?" a polite voice asks.

Uh-oh. As I move around the bend, I see there's a small recessed area with a large white desk sitting in it.

Behind the desk is a big apple-cheeked guy in a green uniform. His nametag says JORDAN.

"No, thanks, I'm fine," I say.

I take another step down the hall.

"Hey, wait," Jordan says. "You can't go down there, you have to sign in first."

I look at him. He's smiling and sipping a cup of coffee.

"Okay," I say, and slowly move toward him.

"Sorry about that," he tells me. "They make me stop everybody."

"Gotta have rules," I answer. "That's what makes the world go round."

The words sound stupid even before they leave my mouth, but Jordan just grins and nods. Is this really the way people talk in offices?

He points to a clipboard on his desk and hands me a pen.

Out of habit, I almost write "Sullivan Stringfellow" but catch myself just in time. I'm trying to think of a name I can use when I notice the small television in the back of Jordan's cubicle. It's on the news, and they're showing footage of a place that looks like it's been hit by an earthquake or a bomb.

The words at the bottom of the screen say "Nitro City Burrito Festival."

"Will you turn that up?" I say.

Jordan hits the volume button.

"The fighting here is fierce and constant, but it's a losing battle," the reporter says. "The park looks like a sea of mutants, and it's only a matter of time before it spills over into the city. We're told preparations are being made for a mass evacuation. The only good news is that former agents of P.L.U.N.G.E., not seen in Nitro City for a generation, have re-emerged and are buying residents precious time. But it's been a costly effort. Ambulances are running nonstop, and local hospitals say they're overwhelmed."

"Big Joe!" I gasp.

"Pardon?" Jordan says.

"Oh...I was just writing my name," I tell him.

"Your name is Big Joe?"

"Uh-huh."

Jordan's still smiling, but it's not as friendly as it was a minute ago.

"I only ask because you don't look, well, big," he says. "And you seem kind of young."

"That's what everybody says," I tell him.

"Uh-huh. I'm going to need to see your ID."

The smile is gone now. I check the pocket of the lab coat.

"Um, I must have left it in my other—"

I drop the pen and bolt down the hallway.

"Stop!" Jordan yells.

He chases after me but, to be real honest, he's not the fastest guard I've ever seen. I head through a set of glass double doors and end up in what appears to be some sort of an office complex. Up ahead, I spot two other security people, so I dash into the nearest men's room.

It's a nice one—roomy, clean, corporate-looking. I open the door to the last stall and step inside.

What am I going to do? My friends are in danger, the city could fall at any minute, and I'm trapped in the bathroom of some secret facility that isn't even supposed to exist. I've got to find Merv, and I've got to do it now!

But I can't leave—the restroom door just opened. I sit on the toilet and lift my legs in the air to hide my feet. When I peek through the small crack by the hinge, I see two men washing their hands. One of them is Harlon Todd, our city's mayor, and the other is Iron-water chairman Herman Wiest.

"Dang it, Herman. I didn't want to say anything in front of the others, but this is not what I agreed to. Our number one tourist event is a disaster. A total disaster! We may have to evacuate. It's all over the news."

"Yes, I know," Mr. Wiest says, his voice as calm as elevator music. "We're getting excellent coverage. It's the top trending story on the internet."

"Excellent?" the mayor snaps. "The whole world is hearing about this."

Herman Wiest turns off the faucet in the sink. He runs a hand through his salt-and-pepper hair and straightens his necktie.

"Exactly," he says. "You see, Mayor, a big public event is the perfect time to remind our customers what we protect them from each and every day. And not just our customers here—also the ones in New York, Los Angeles, Paris, London, Rome. Everywhere. An event like this scares cities around the world. And they're willing to pay to feel safe again."

"And if people get hurt?"

"Then they'll pay more," Mr. Wiest says.

Wow. He sure seems a lot nicer in his TV commercials.

"Relax, Harlon. We'll blame P.L.U.N.G.E. the way we blame them for everything. And in the end, Ironwater will be the company that saved the day. Now go back to the meeting. I'm going to be a minute."

Mayor Todd looks like he's about to say something, then stares at the floor. Without another word, he leaves.

Herman Wiest turns around and walks right toward me. My whole body goes stiff. The next few seconds are agonizing, but then I hear him go into the stall right next door to mine. I stay perfectly still on my perch and try not to breathe…for a lot of reasons.

BAM!

The restroom door bursts wide open.

"All right, you filthy, stinkin' sack of slime," Jordan roars. "Fun's over. Come on out of there!"

The silence is awkward.

"You want me to come out *now?*" Mr. Wiest says.

You can actually hear the blood rushing out of Jordan's face.

"Mr. Wiest!" he says. "I am so, so sorry. I didn't know it was you. Honestly, if I'd known, then I'd never, ever…it's just that I'm looking for this kid, and I thought he might have come in here."

"A kid? What kid?"

"That's just it, sir. I don't know. I mean, he looked like a kid, but he was wearing a lab coat, and you know, some of those geniuses are pretty young, and I was only doing my job. But then he wouldn't give me his name. Which is so weird because that never happens. I mean, of course it never happens, not here, because there's no way anyone can get in. Anyway, he ran off down the hall, but I'll find him, sir."

"See that you do."

"Oh, I will. Absolutely. Don't you worry about a thing, Mr. Wiest. Just enjoy your...I'm going to go now."

The door clunks closed as Jordan makes a hasty backward exit.

I let out a long quiet sigh of relief and reposition myself on the toilet. When I do, my backpack tilts, and I watch in horror as something flat with little plastic fingers falls out of the pouch and crashes against the floor tiles.

It's my scratchula.

"Scratchula—it's the spatula that scratches your back!" my mom explained when she gave it to me. "They're going to be huge!"

Thanks, Mom. Thanks a lot.

I close my eyes and wait for the metal door in front of me to open. But it doesn't. And as far as I can tell, nothing's happening next door. Maybe he didn't hear it? It's possible. I'm sure it seemed louder on my side. Still, he might see it. I mean, it's sitting there just inches from the divider that separates our tiny rooms.

Like a toilet-climbing cat burglar, I stealthily lean forward and lower my hand to the floor. Suddenly, another hand darts under the divider and grabs my arm! His grip is strong and I lose my balance, tumbling onto the tile. I stare under the divider, but all I can see are shoes covered by a pretty nice pair of pants. I rip my arm away and that's when I notice something else—something that makes my heart race like a drumroll.

Herman Wiest has a scar just below his left knee.

Chapter 41

Saturday, 6:21 p.m.

Something the Moleman told me echoes through my brain.

"The Midnight Flush bit H.W. just below the knee. It left a nasty scar."

It's nasty, all right.

Terrified, I shimmy under the stall door and fly out of the bathroom like a rocket. I'm two steps down the hall when I spy a security guard cruising toward me in something that looks like a long, topless golf cart. I whirl around so that my back is to him, but I hear the cart come to a stop. I'm done for.

"Security!" Herman Wiest's voice screams from inside the restroom. "Security!"

Instantly, the guard leaps off the cart and runs through the door. It's a lucky break. Unfortunately, it might not matter. Down the hall, Jordan is headed this way, and he's bringing friends.

I jump onto the abandoned cart, turn the wheel, and streak down the hallway.

"Stop him! Stop that cart!" Jordan yells.

All around me, office doors are popping open like jack-in-the-box lids. People step out of them just long enough to dive out of my way. I'm driving through a rain of papers, file folders, and white foam coffee cups flung into the air by horrified clerks. There's a curve up ahead. I veer around it at top speed, proving once and for all that the weekend I spent at go-kart camp was not for nothing.

Glancing back, I see that Jordan and his security team are in hot pursuit, along with a mob of angry office workers. I've got no clue where I'm going. My only plan is to keep moving down the long, mazelike hallway until an idea hits me.

WHAM!

That wasn't an idea. As I run through a hallway intersection, my cart is broadsided by a vehicle that could be its twin. I fight the wheel, swerving one way, then the other, and barely avoid crashing into the wall. The large, broad-shouldered driver pulls up beside me. He's wearing a blue shirt, meaning he's an Ick, and I see a gold front tooth shining in his mouth. He jerks his steering wheel to the right, smashing his cart against mine, then gives me a menacing grin.

He swerves and rams me again. I steer my cart to the right, then bring it back hard to the left, bashing it against Gold Tooth. That wipes the smile off his face. We're neck and neck racing through the halls, clipping each other like bumper-car warriors. The big goon glares at me and I glare back, but something catches the corner of my eye. I risk a quick peek at the road ahead and...uh-oh.

There's a turn. A sharp, square-edged, right-angle turn that leads to another hallway. And it's coming up fast. Quickly, I punch the accelerator, swing wide, and yank the cart back again. It fishtails, catching Gold Tooth's front wheels. I see fear in his eyes and hear the brakes squeal, but it's too late.

He careens into a vending machine, sending an avalanche of soda cans streaming into the hall. I'm practically on two wheels when I make the turn, but I make it.

Only there's nowhere to go.

Dead ahead of me is the end of the line. Two thick, sturdy steel doors block any hope of escape. I steer away and slam on the brakes. The cart spins sideways and crashes against the side wall.

I'm dazed, but there's no time to gather my senses. The mob has just rounded the corner at the end of the hall.

"There he is!" Jordan yells.

They let out what sounds to me like a war cry, and break into a run.

I climb out of the cart and blaze through one of the big steel doors. There's a push broom propped against the wall. I grab it and jam the stick through the two C-shaped door handles. Quickly, I whirl around and—

"Whoa," I gasp.

What I see is unlike anything I have ever seen before. I'm standing on a large, half-moon-shaped balcony that looks out into plumbing heaven. I walk over to the glass railing and stare. I am at least five stories in the air, gazing out at a gigantic cavern filled with pipes, tubes, valves, fittings, flanges, and connections that seem to go on forever. Up above my head, I see pipelines crisscrossing each other like threads in a spiderweb. Down below me there's a maze of catwalks hovering over forklifts, cranes, trucks, and a small army of people in hardhats busy doing, well, whatever it is they do down there.

I'm in the nerve center of the Nitrodome. The place the plumbers call the heart of the Underworld.

Even considering the desperateness of my situation, it's a great view...until I look to my left, anyway. Just across the left railing, bursting out of the wall, is a row of mega-sized, mega-ugly chrome-plated letters.

They spell IRONWATER.

Chapter 42

Saturday, 6:45 p.m.

BAM!

Something rams against the steel doors from the other side.

BAM!

The hit is harder this time, and the broom handle cracks in half. A horde of angry faces comes rushing through.

I don't think, I just react. Climbing over the rail, I take a deep breath and leap out into the nothingness. My feet land on top of the big metal "I" in the

Ironwater sign. I glue my back to the wall and try very, very hard not to look down.

"Come back here!" Jordan yells. "You're going to fall!"

To be fair, he seems genuinely concerned. I can't say the same for some of the other mobsters. The balcony is crowded now, and I see a dozen hands reaching for me.

Whether they're trying to help or to push, I'm not exactly sure. But to be on the safe side, I leap to the letter "R."

This gets a nervous roar from the crowd.

"Go away. Just leave me alone!" I tell them.

But they don't go away. They do, however, move to the sides, splitting into two halves like a perfectly sliced sandwich. A tall, slim man with salt-and-pepper hair, gray slacks, and a red tie walks through the opening. Calmly, Herman Wiest takes off his sports coat, hands it to Jordan, and hops over the rail.

Then, with the grace of a young deer, he leaps onto the "I."

"So, tell me," he says, "what's a nice kid like you doing in a place like this?"

I was just wondering the same thing myself. I turn

around and jump to the "O." Before I can even steady myself, Herman Wiest is on the "R."

"You don't have to do this," I tell him. "I mean, I don't know anything."

"Know anything about what?" he says.

His eyes are black and shiny. He watches me like a cat watches a caged bird.

"About anything," I say.

I make it to the "N."

"Well, then you must be curious," he tells me.

"Not really."

"Indulge me," he says, and moves a letter nearer. "You see, from the time they first crawled out of the sewage, mutants have been unpredictable creatures. You just never knew what was going to emerge from that oozing slime. Fortunately, here under the dome, we've been able to correct that. The mutants we're creating are bigger, stronger, and much more destructive than your typical sewer monster. Why, our scientists have come up with an eel that—well, let's just say that the first time I saw it, I nearly peed my pants."

"Congratulations," I say.

I jump onto the "W."

"You see, I've known for a long time that the

mutants were the key to controlling the sewers. And, as I'm sure you've heard, he who controls the sewers controls everything."

He moves to the "N" like he's strolling through a park.

"That's none of my business," I tell him. "I'm only here to find some master valve that's supposed to reset the whole sewer system."

"Oh, you must mean that one," he says, pointing upward.

And there it is. There's Merv. I'd know it anywhere, glistening and gold and huge. It's high up in the air, hidden among the jungle of pipes and valves that fill the dome.

"So that valve resets the entire system?" Mr. Wiest says. "Interesting. I've always wondered what it did. It doesn't look like anything else in the sewer. It's been up there for decades. I wonder if it even works anymore. Pity you won't be able to find out. Still, it's always nice to see a piece of history."

He leaps onto the "W." I'm taking no chances— I jump to the "A" and instantly move on to the "T." He makes another bound, staying one letter behind me.

"Look, it's not too late," I tell him. "All you have to do is open the valve. I'll give you all the credit. You can be the hero. You can save the city."

He joins me on the "T."

"Why would I want to do that?" he asks.

I see it now—I see it in his eyes. This was never about drumming up business for Ironwater. From the beginning, he's meant to destroy the city.

I move to the far edge of the letter.

"Let's stop playing games, Sullivan Stringfellow. I know who you are, I know who your grandfather is, and you know perfectly well who I am."

"I won't tell anybody you're the Human Waste," I say.

He smiles.

"No. You won't," he says. "Not that it would matter much. Very soon, the world will know that the Human Waste is back. And he's bigger than ever. There are no troublesome P.L.U.N.G.E. agents to stop me this time. Only you."

I leap to the letter "E." He's right behind me.

"I have to admit, I'm disappointed," he says. "Imagine them sending a child. I'd hoped for more of a challenge. Don't misunderstand, it's not your fault. It's just, well, I'm a super-criminal, the best of the worst. And I have all of this."

He holds out his arm, showing me the terrible awesomeness of the Nitrodome. I make one last, desperate leap onto the giant "R." I'm out of letters, and out of time.

The Human Waste gives me a slow, sad headshake.

"But you? You're just a boy. What do you have?"

I glance down at the ground below me and feel a little dizzy. Carefully, I reach into my backpack and pull out a silver-and-black plastic casing.

"I have this," I say quietly.

He stares at it and frowns.

"You have a drain snake?" he says.

I nod.

"You're telling me you have a drain snake? And just what do you intend to do with that?"

I glare into his cold, dark eyes.

"Save the day," I say.

Chapter 43

Saturday, 6:58 p.m.

I lift my arm and fire. The claw on the end of the Mole-man's amazing retractable drain snake soars through the air like a missile. It wraps itself around an overhead pipe, and like Tarzan on a vine, I swing down to the metal catwalk below.

"Get him! Get that boy!" Herman Wiest screams.

I push a button, and the long, flexible cable returns to its casing. Instantly, I turn and run toward the metal ladder that will take me up to Merv's level, but a freckle-faced, green-shirted guard gets there first.

"I've got you," Freckles says, blocking my path. "Give up, kid, there's nowhere to go."

When I turn around, two more green-shirts are rushing down the catwalk. Everywhere I look, guards are cutting off my exits and clanking up flights of industrial stairs. The net is tightening around me.

With no other option, I raise my arm and fire the drain snake straight into the air.

It snares a pipe, one that's nowhere near where I need to be, but it'll have to do. Quickly, I press the Retract button and feel myself streaking skyward. I'm pulled higher and higher toward the endless network of pipes filling the space above me like branches in a forest. As I move upward, the angry voices below fade to whispers, and it looks like I just might make it.

But looks are deceiving. Out of nowhere, I see the tall steel boom of a construction crane swinging toward me. Someone is dangling from the end of it—it's Gold Tooth. He reaches for me, but I kick at his arms and he backs away. I grab on to an overhead pipe and pull myself forward. When I do, the claw on the drain snake releases, and I watch the Moleman's invention make the long, long fall to the ground below.

It smashes against the concrete floor.

"Hey, kid," Gold Tooth yells, pointing at the ground. "You're next."

Quickly, I make a desperate grab for another pipe, and another one after that, moving hand over hand across them like a set of monkey bars. When the crane is close enough, Gold Tooth leaps out and snags a pipe with his hand, climbing after me.

Fortunately, I'm almost to the ladder, just one jump to go—but it's a big one. I put both hands on the pipe, swing back and forth a couple of times, then release it. In that instant, I'm airborne, sailing through space with nothing beneath me. There's a sudden stop, and I feel my toes land on something solid—a skinny metal rung on the ladder. My hands clutch frantically for a hold, and just as I'm tilting backward, my index finger catches the inside rail. Somehow, I manage to throw my weight forward and get a grip.

Steady, Sully, steady. It's a miracle I've made it this far. I give a long, grateful sigh and start to climb.

A minute later, I reach the narrow platform that will take me to Merv. I look down—Gold Tooth is streaking up the ladder like an express elevator.

As fast as I can, I race to the large gold valve, pull the key from around my neck, put it into the slot, and twist. Then I grab the massive wheel and pull down hard.

It doesn't budge.

Gold Tooth is halfway up the ladder. I pull again.

Still nothing. He's nearly to the platform.

I twist my shoulders and throw my weight into it, and—suddenly—it gives. The wheel creaks, and I roll it as far as I can. The valve is open!

Only...nothing happens.

The Ick steps out onto the metal floor and moves toward me. His golden grin is in full view.

"That was your plan?" he says, the smugness in his voice as thick as frozen ketchup. "I could've told you it was never gonna work. That valve's an antique. I don't think these pipes are even connected anymore. Which means you did all of this for nothin', kid. So if I were you, I'd just come on back down nice and quiet."

It doesn't look like I have a choice. Merv didn't work, and I'm out of options. I take a step toward Gold Tooth, and then stop. What's that sound? It's like a hissing, popping, rumbling noise. Suddenly, I realize what it is—and so does Gold Tooth. His eyes bulge out like snow globes.

"If I were you," I tell him, "I'd hold my breath."

A river of liquid explodes out of the pipe! It's powerful, like a fire hose, and it hits me square in the chest.
I fall back into Gold Tooth, and the stream pushes us
both off the platform. We land hard on a metal catwalk
fifteen feet below. The impact knocks the breath out of
me, but after a minute, I try to get to my feet. It's no
use—water is bursting from pipes all around me, forcing me back down. I hear a creaking noise, and the
catwalk starts to sway. The strong current snaps the
supports, and one side of the walkway collapses. I slide
down the metal grate and feel myself falling through
air, and then—

WHAP!

I land on a tall stack of cardboard boxes on the floor
of the Nitrodome. There's a groaning sound behind
me, and when I lift my head, I see Gold Tooth lying
flat on his belly a few feet away. Valves in every part of
the room are bursting open, spewing out great green
waterfalls of yuck.

"What the..."

It finally occurs to me what's happening—and why
the plumbers were so sure this would work. Merv isn't
just a valve—it opens every valve in the sewer. We are
inside the most powerful flush of all time. Gold Tooth

rises to his knees on the mountain of boxes, mumbling to himself. He looks around the room, and then his eyes fall on me. I try to move—but I can't. My leg is wedged between two heavy boxes. I'm caught like a mouse in a trap.

And that's when the double doors swing open.

"Everyone out! Out! Out!" an agitated woman in a green uniform yells. "We're evacuating!"

"Evacuating where?" someone asks.

"To the surface. The dome is collapsing."

I hear mass panic below as a mob rushes for the exit.

Gold Tooth seems dazed, and he stares blankly at the scrambling figures below. His wrench has landed next to him. He picks it up, gets to his feet, then moves toward me. I push against the boxes with both hands, but I can't free my leg. Then there's a squawk from a loudspeaker, and a recorded message plays again and again.

"Evacuate. Evacuate. Evacuate."

It's a disturbing sound, like an alarm clock you can't shut off.

But Gold Tooth isn't listening. He takes another step toward me, growls, and raises the wrench.

WHACK!

A large piece of metal catwalk crashes onto the pile of boxes. They spring up like a catapult, launching Gold Tooth into the air.

He shoots upward like a cannonball, then splashes down in the swirling muck below.

A minute later, I see him leave, the last Ironwater worker to make his way through the double doors.

"Evacuate. Evacuate. Evacuate."

They can shut that off now. There's no one here but me.

And I'm not going anywhere.

Chapter 44

Saturday, 7:40 p.m.

I lie back and try to imagine the celebration they'll have down at the Golden Poo. There'll be chili burgers, egg creams, and pie—real pie this time, not just a password. Who knows? They might even give me a twenty-one-flush salute. It's the traditional send-off when plumbers lose one of their own.

I mean, I know I'm not really one of their own, but still. The thought of the old legends standing around the toilet saying nice stuff about me—it almost makes the whole thing worth it.

The water is most of the way up the pile of boxes now. I've got to hand it to Merv—he works fast. I give my leg one last yank, but it's useless because…

It moved. I felt it, it moved! Of course—the water! What was I thinking? Water floats whales and cruise ships, it can definitely handle a bunch of stupid boxes.

I wait for the water to rise a little higher, then push with everything I've got. I feel it loosening, but I'm still stuck. I need—I don't know—a tool, a wedge, something! But there's nothing, at least nothing I can reach. The only things nearby are some wet cardboard boxes, an English paper that fell out of my backpack, the stupid hatula my mom sent me, an old—

Wait a second…the hatula! I stretch as far as I can and get a finger on the brim, then drag it toward me. Using the spatula as a lever, I try to pry the two boxes apart. It doesn't give me much, but I don't need much. I hear a sound like I'm pulling my foot out of a bucket of wet cement, and after one last tug—I'm free! I jump into the water and swim for the double doors, but a heavy beam is jammed up against them. When I move it out of the way, a powerful wave bursts through the doors and pushes me across the room. I'm caught in the current, and I can't stop myself. Reaching out, I grab the back of a floating forklift, and together we smash through the giant ventilation fan on the far wall.

Suddenly, I find myself plunging three stories into an ocean that wasn't here when I arrived. The nine-thousand-pound forklift crashes through the water, and the suction takes me down with it. When I reach the bottom, I see a steel grate like the one where the men were dumping the barrels of Muta-Nix. Only this gate is wide open, hanging by one hinge. If any slithery creatures were behind it, they're not there now.

Which means they're out here. With me.

I stick my head out of the water and gasp for air. Anything could be in the muck around me. Anything. I spot a large flat sign floating by and grab hold of it. Kicking my legs, I try to move forward, but for some reason, I end up farther back than when I started.

And I'm picking up pretty good speed, too. What's going on? I look back over my shoulder—and instantly wish I hadn't. A huge whirlpool, spinning like a drain, is pulling in everything around it.

I maneuver myself toward a fallen support beam that's sticking up out of the water like a shipwreck. Making a desperate grab, I snag it, stopping my momentum. Now if I can only—

I stop thinking. Or breathing. Or doing anything at all. Because as much as I'd like to move, I'm paralyzed by the sight I see directly in front of me.

It's an eel. An eel the size of a dragon. I understand now why this creature would make Herman Wiest pee his pants. I understand better than I care to admit.

It comes out of the water like the periscope of a submarine, rising higher and higher, until it looks like a wood carving on the front of a Viking ship. Its cold red eyes look down on me, and when its mouth opens, I see fangs the size of fence pickets. Its neck curls, and the eel thrusts its massive head toward me. I brace myself for the impact—and that's when the creature gets hit by the truck.

Really—an honest-to-goodness truck. I think I'm just as surprised as the eel is. I'd have to say this is pretty much the last place on Earth you'd expect to see a traffic accident. I mean, I'm the only person around for miles, and I don't even have a driver's license.

It's one of the black-and-green cargo trucks I saw in the garage. It was caught in the current and being pulled into the spinning funnel when it collided with the dragon. I see the creature floating motionless toward the whirlpool. Then it disappears into the foamy void.

I'm relieved—not that it makes a whole lot of difference. Because I can't hold on any longer. Not another second. I try, but the current is just too strong, and when I let go, the whirlpool spins me around and around until everything goes black. I'm pulled under the dark, murky water.

And then I'm up again. What just happened? I find myself moving away from the spinning sinkhole of death, even though I'm not doing a thing to make it happen. What's even stranger is that all of a sudden I have the weirdest sense that I'm not alone.

And then I see it. An enormous gray back arches, and I feel myself rising up into the air, then slowly moving down again.

I don't know exactly what I'm sitting on. All I know is that I'm clinging to it for dear life. If I had to guess— and it's only a guess—I'd say this is a giant earthworm, maybe twenty-five or thirty feet long. It moves up and down, as if it were wriggling across a table. I can see a head—or what I assume is a head—emerging a few feet in front of me before disappearing back under the water. My hands are locked on to the ridges in the smooth, rubbery flesh.

We pull away from the current, and the worm skims

along the surface, making a wide circle around the dome. But as thrilling as this moment is, it only confirms what Max knew from the beginning. This was a one-way trip. There's no way out of here, not for me. If the others escaped, they left no sign of their exit. Meanwhile, pieces of dome are falling all around me. I should be terrified, and I am, but not for the reason I'd expect. I'm terrified about what's happening up there in the real world. Did it work? Is the city still here? Did the plumbers hold the linc?

Is Big Joe all right? Is Max?

I'll never know. But I'd like to think I made a difference. I tilt my head back and close my eyes, feeling the breeze and the spray as we arch and dive, arch and dive.

When I open my eyes again, I see the wreckage of Ironwater, and the rising muck, and something else—something that wasn't there a minute ago.

I see one of Tiny's sewer angels.

I don't know what else I would call her. She looks about my age, or maybe a little older. She has long, light-brown hair that's tied in a braid, but probably the most interesting thing about her is where she is.

She's on the ceiling—watching from above.

I blink my eyes because I can't believe it. Her arms and legs are spread out wide like a lizard's, and she's clinging to the top of the dome. She crawls across it as easily as I walk across a floor, and if I make it out of here, I will never doubt another word Tiny Dinkins says ever again.

"Hello!" I yell. "Hello up there!"

The girl doesn't answer, she just stops and extends her arm. I can't imagine what she's doing. But after a few seconds, it becomes clear. She's pointing.

I follow her finger to an odd, distorted patch in the roof of the dome. Nothing appears to be there, and yet I'm absolutely sure something is there.

The closest I can come to describing it is to say it's like one of those magic 3-D pictures. You know, the ones you can't see on the page until you take your eyes out of focus, and then they pop out at you, and you wonder why you didn't see them before.

I see it now. I see it clearly. She's pointing to the invisible door.

The invisible door is an old plumber's tale that's been around for as long as there's been a Nitrodome. According to the story, when the place was being built,

Ironwater wanted a solid, completely sealed dome. But the workers got nervous, thinking a cave-in could trap them inside. So they secretly installed a hidden exit— one Ironwater wouldn't see.

I never believed the story—why would I? Then again, I'm seeing a lot of things I didn't believe before.

"Thank you!" I yell, then close my eyes and scream as loud as I can, "THANNNK YOOOOOOOU!"

But when I open them again, the angel who appeared out of nowhere is gone.

Chapter 45

Saturday, 8:22 p.m.

Now that I know where the invisible door is, there's only one problem—reaching it.

I look for a way up, but there's nothing. *Think, Sully.* If I were going to build an invisible door, how would I get to it? Simple—invisible ladder. It's the only thing that makes sense.

I give the earthworm a last, grateful pat, and dive into the water. Swimming until I reach the wall, I find the area directly below the door. I feel along the smooth surface—there's a small indentation. It's not much, just enough to slip my fingers inside, but it's there. I move my hand higher and find there's one above it, and one above that, and one above that. And my gut tells me they lead all the way to the door.

At first, the climb is easy, but the farther I go, the less I'm crawling up, and the more I'm crawling sideways. When I'm practically parallel with the ground, I see the door just a few feet in front of me. From here, it's plain as day, and my heart starts to race. I reach out for the final stretch, but my feet slip, and I find myself hanging in space by one arm. And it's a long, long way to the water below me.

I swing my body forward and—with just the tips of my fingers—get a grip on the door.

There's a small slot with a lever in it. One quick squeeze and the hatch bursts open like a pimple on a big metal forehead. I grab hold and pull myself inside.

The inside is…not what I expected. I thought I'd be crawling out into daylight, but so far I'm in total darkness. I keep moving ahead, thinking something must be around the next turn, but there's just more nothing. I keep crawling. It feels like an hour has passed, and my knees are raw and bleeding, but I'm convinced there has to be a light at the end of the tunnel.

The tunnel makes a sharp turn upward, and I still can't see where it ends. All I can do is keep climbing, and climbing, and—

CLANK!

Ow! My head rams into something. Something hard. Don't tell me this is a dead end! I reach up and feel around in the dark—it's a metal hatch. And when I open it, the entire tunnel is filled with warm, glorious light!

Grabbing both sides of the portal, I pull myself out of the hole.

When I do, the first thing I see is another hole. Only it's not a hole. It's a nostril. It is the single largest nostril I personally have ever stared into, and to be real honest, I'm a little freaked out. Then I realize I'm not just looking up any nose—I'm looking up Captain Clog's nose. This is Mount Flushmore. I'm at the Burrito Festival!

Like a meerkat on guard duty, I stick my head out of the big stone toilet and look around.

There's a crowd. I didn't expect that. I don't know what I expected, but I didn't think there'd still be people milling around the grounds. Plumbers, sure, but not people. I wouldn't call it a festival crowd—it's not nearly big enough, or happy enough, and nobody's eating. These people look like they've been through a war.

Actually, the whole place does. There's no music because the bandstand is smashed. The rides are toppled over. The booths, the ones that ought to be making the most incredible burritos ever, are strewn all over the park.

It takes every ounce of strength I have, but I manage to crawl out of the bowl and park myself on the rim.

As I sit here on the giant toilet—in hindsight, not the best pose I could've chosen—I notice a few people are starting to point up at me. They don't look surprised, just curious. But before long, a crowd starts to gather. The first person I actually recognize is Tank Huberman, only I don't think he knows it's me. Then after a few seconds, his face turns pale, and his eyes bulge out, and his big fat burrito hole falls wide open.

"Oh, my gosh," he gasps. "It can't be!"

He breaks into a wide smile.

"Somebody go get Joe!" he yells.

The crowd goes into a frenzy. They swarm around Mount Flushmore, cheering and shouting. People I don't even know are calling out my name. The look of devastation I saw on the faces just a few minutes ago is gone. Now there's excitement. It's almost like the festival is still going on. Plumbers start to gather around, great plumbers I've looked up to my whole life. And now here they are, clapping…clapping for me.

I'm pretty sure this must be a dream.

But if it is, I need to wake up. I need to wake up now. Because the cheers coming from the crowd turn to screams, and I can see the horror on every face staring up at me.

Before I even turn around, I know what's happened. I didn't close the invisible door. It never even occurred to me. Why would it? The Nitrodome was destroyed, the nightmare was over. But looking back, I really wish I had.

Because the dragon eel, the one I saw spiraling into the whirlpool, is right behind me.

I turn just in time to see the enormous ugly head snaking up from the toilet.

"Get out of there!" Tank yells.

Leaping off the rim, I scramble down the hill and fall onto the pavement. The dragon eel slithers forward.

Instinctively, the people move back, and I find myself alone at the foot of Mount Flushmore. Suddenly, a motorcycle bursts through the crowd. One-Eyed Lily Cruz pulls alongside me, and I see Izzy on the back.

"Take this!" she yells, tossing me something.

I catch the Moleman's Party Pooper 3000 and, in one motion, turn and throw the powerful plunger like a javelin. I watch it fly into the air, rise upward—and sail just above the dragon eel's head.

The crowd gasps.

"You missed!" Izzy yells.

But I didn't miss. I hit exactly what I was aiming for—Wild Bill Sullivan's nose. The plunger sticks, hanging there like the best part of a Pinocchio costume, and then...

BOOOOOOOOM!

The explosion is large, loud, and everything the Moleman promised it would be. Mount Flushmore collapses into a pile of rubble, burying the dragon eel beneath it.

My ears are ringing from the blast. I walk out of the swirling dust cloud and stare into a sea of stunned, silent faces.

And then they mob me.

Howling and cheering, the crowd rushes forward, smothering me in a gargantuan group hug.

"Let me through! Let me through!"

Big Joe pushes his way through the crowd. He's smiling, something that's probably only happened a handful of times in his whole life, and I'm a little worried his face can't take the stress.

Tiny Dinkins is beside him, and together they lift me onto their shoulders. They carry me through the sea of people, and dozens of plumbers rush up to shake my hand.

When they put me down, it's behind a long white car that says NITRO CITY AMBULANCE on the door. It's only then that I realize how badly I hurt. I have more bruises than I have space on my body. I'm so tired I can barely stand.

The door to the ambulance swings open, and that's when I see it's already occupied. Slowly, a mauled and battered figure emerges from the back.

"I'll get the next one," Max Bleeker tells me. "This one's for heroes."

Chapter 46

Tuesday, 3:19 p.m.
Seventeen days since the Burrito Festival

Mom and Dad and Emmy are headed back to Fiji on Saturday. I know I'm going to miss them—I sort of do already—but I won't miss the hovering. It's like I'm made of glass or something. The worst part was that first week, when I was in the hospital and still had a bunch of tubes and lines coming out of me. Mom was crying all the time, and Dad looked sick to his stomach, and Emmy—well, Emmy seemed fine.

I had to keep checking to see if she was unplugging my machines.

"The doctor says you're going to be all right, son," dad said on the first night they arrived.

I already knew that, of course. I was pretty banged up, but no permanent damage. Still, just hearing it from my dad—and in his actual voice, not coming out of the speaker of my laptop—made me feel a lot better.

"We are never leaving you alone again. Not for a second," my mom said, tears rolling down her face like a faucet left on too long.

She pulled a tissue out of the handle of a long silver spatula.

"Oh, it's got a removable plastic compartment where you can store anything you want to keep handy. Tissues, pencils, keys, spices—anything. We call it a this-and-that-ula," she said, then started to wail again. "It's going to be huge!"

A lot of kids from my school came to visit me in the hospital. I hated that part. It was like a very boring slumber party where I was the only one wearing pajamas. Of course, I knew some people would come, like Nixon. We talked a little. I let him eat my lime Jell-O. He also ate my pot roast, potatoes, hot roll, and apple pie. I didn't want him to, but he's quicker than he looks, and I was too weak to stop him.

"Did you hear April's transferring to Basher Academy?" he asked me.

"Basher? Wow," I said.

It's a tough institution. From a kid's perspective, it's pretty much the worst punishment out there.

"I've heard they can break anybody," Nixon said. "They're used to handling the really hard cases, the baddest of the bad...Ten bucks says she's running the place by the end of the year."

I didn't take the bet because I had a feeling he was right. Even now, it sends a chill down my spine. I mean, it's a military school—they've probably got weapons.

After Nixon left, Leonard showed up. That wasn't too bad because it wasn't the real Leonard. I'm convinced of that. It was like a robot version of Leonard, an automated principal that you wind up and he tells your parents awesome things about you. It was total baloney, but he did it with so much enthusiasm that I'm a little surprised they haven't named the school after me.

But of all the visits, I'd have to say the strangest was Izzy's. For starters, she brought me a cactus. What kind of a person brings a dangerous, pointy, spiky porcupine-of-the-desert to someone in the hospital? For all she knows, that could be how a lot of people ended up there in the first place.

Her long black hair was pulled back into a ponytail, and she wore yellow jeans and a T-shirt that said SMILE. IT'LL MAKE PEOPLE WONDER WHAT YOU'RE UP TO.

"I want you to know I'm only here because they're giving extra credit to people who come see you in the hospital," she said.

Hmmmmm...I wondered why I was getting so many visitors.

"Fine," I told her. "You visited. You can leave now."

For a moment, I thought she was going to, but then she gave me a long, probing look.

"I better stick around a few minutes. There might be a test or something," she said. "How much pain are you in?"

"Normally, or just since you got here?"

She glared at me. Then she walked over and sat in a chair by the bed.

"So what are you going to do now? I mean, when you get out of the hospital. Is military school still on the table?"

"No," I snapped.

"Are you sure?" she said, then turned to look at my mom. "There's really no better place for him to get the structure and discipline he needs."

"Actually, we haven't decided what we're going to do when Sully gets out," Mom explained. "We were thinking it might be nice for him to come live with us in Fiji. Or we might move back here. Some of Sully's old schools have indicated a willingness to be a little more…understanding about his past difficulties."

For just a fraction of a second, I thought I saw Izzy's eyelids twitch, almost like the news bothered her. But it could've been all the medication they were pumping into me.

"Well, it's none of my business," she said. "Of course, if you wanted to, I guess you could leave him at Gloomy Valley. I mean, we're used to him there. The shock has kind of worn off. And who knows what would happen at a new school? He's not the most stable person, you know."

"I'll keep that in mind," Mom said.

Izzy turned around to face me.

"I guess you think you're a pretty big thing now," she said.

"No."

She shrugged.

"Some of the kids at school, they think you're a big thing. Not me, of course."

"Of course," I said.

"But, well, I will say this," she started, and I could tell she was having a hard time getting the words out. "When it came right down to it and everything was on the line, you didn't stink as much as I thought you would."

"I know. That's what you wrote on my get-well card."

She nods.

"Well, I guess that's about it then. If anyone asks, tell them I visited."

"It's all I'll be talking about," I said.

She scowled at me and turned to leave.

"Oh, and just so you know, that prom thing is still on. A deal's a deal."

I swallowed hard, and I think my heart monitor started beeping.

"But it's only if you can't find somebody else, right?" I plead. "And I mean *anybody* else?"

She gave me a twisted, evil grin.

"We'll see, sewer boy. We'll see."

She left, and for a minute, the whole room was filled with an awkward silence. Finally, my mom spoke.

"Lovely girl," she said. "Do you have any human friends?"

Thursday, 7:15 p.m.
Nineteen days since the Burrito Festival

"Well, well, well, if it isn't the dragon slayer," Tank says.

After what happened at the Burrito Festival, I got the nickname dragon slayer—and kept it for almost five minutes. Now I'm just the kid who wrecked Mount Flushmore. When people found out how much it was going to cost to rebuild it, I went from hero to bad guy in nothing flat.

Needless to say, the Moleman is thrilled.

That's okay. I mean, it's not like we don't already have plenty of herocs from that day, most of them right here in the Golden Poo. From what I've heard, the plumbers were amazing. Picture this: the festival is in a complete meltdown—hideous, nauseating sewer monsters are coming out of toilets, sinks, fountains, gutters…well, basically anywhere there's a hole in the ground. I've heard stories about rescues, and battling packs of sewer rats, and taking back bathrooms anyone in their right mind would have given up for lost. But the strange thing is, I haven't heard them from the plumbers.

From what I can tell, to them, this was just another day on the job.

The Golden Age must have been really something.

This is my third time being back at the Poo since I got out of the hospital. The first time, everybody made a big deal about it, and the second time, some people still crowded around me, but now things are more or less back to normal. And that's the way it ought to be.

"Hey Joe...look!" Molly Cannon yells, pointing straight up. "There's somebody walking around on the ceiling!"

Everybody laughs—everybody but me. I've heard that joke a few times now, and it's not getting any funnier. I get it, no one believes I saw a sewer angel crawling on the dome, they think I'm crazy. Well, not crazy, just full of—

"Sewer gas," Tank says. "It'll get you every time. We

used to see all kinds of things in the Underworld—lizard people, snake people, frog people..."

"I saw a cat that could talk," Tiny says.

The whole place groans. Big Joe rolls his eyes.

"We've told you a thousand times, Tiny, that cat couldn't talk. He just had a weird meow."

"He could say 'Melvin,'" Tiny says, taking a bite of his pie.

I want to believe him, I really do, because I promised if I made it out of the dome, I'd never question anything Tiny has to say again. But I'll be honest—the fact that Tiny's real name is Melvin doesn't do a lot for his credibility.

"The point is, sewer gas messes with your brain," Tank says. "You stay down too long, you're going to see something freaky. I know a couple of guys who swear they saw a whole Undercity down there. Can you imagine? Of course, those guys weren't too bright to start with."

Maybe Tank is right. Maybe there wasn't any girl, and I didn't ride a giant earthworm, and the whole thing was nothing but a gas-fueled hallucination. But they all saw the dragon eel, and the Nitrodome is a big underground pile of garbage. So if everybody agrees that the terrible stuff I went through was real, why do they think I imagined the good parts?

I take a bite of my chili burger, and it tastes even better than it did before. Big Joe says that's because I earned it. He sucks the ketchup off a French fry, then flings the worthless part onto the counter.

"So what happens now?" I say.

He shrugs.

"The deck gets reshuffled," he says. "It'll take a while for the papers to be filed, but we're hearing the city is going to revoke the law that made plumbing illegal. So some of us may be back on the job—legitimately back on the job—real soon. Right now, Ironwater is still in control, but they're on their way out. Your friend, the one with the eye patch—"

"Lily Cruz," I say.

"Yeah. Turns out she's been investigating them all along. From what I hear, she's got enough on Ironwater to put their top people away for a long time. The mayor, too. Did you know she was with the Secret Sewer Service?"

I nod. Joe lets out a long sigh.

"Who'd have believed it? An S.S.S. agent...in leather pants."

Saturday, 9:40 a.m.
Twenty-one days since the Burrito Festival

I don't like airports. There are too many lines, and too many people, and as far as I'm concerned, way too many good-byes.

My dad comes back from the snack bar. He hands my mom a water, and Emmy a juice box, and I get my personal favorite, grape soda. Mom looks at me, and the tears start to flow.

Hers, I mean. Maybe I'm a little misty, but that's just so she doesn't feel self-conscious.

She touches my face.

"My boy," she says. "My sweet, sweet boy. Now promise me you won't blow up any more janitors."

"I'll try," I tell her.

"That's all I can ask."

She smiles, and it's sad and happy at the same time.

"Now, I hope you'll give some serious thought to

joining the debate team. Who knows, you might be a natural-born lawyer? They work in a nice, safe, clean courtroom," she says, and then her eyes soften. "Look, I'm not saying you have to go to law school, or accounting school, or anything. I'm just saying it's something to fall back on if this plumber thing...well, if it ever goes away."

I know she wishes it would, but still, this is the closest she's ever come to accepting that it's more than a phase.

I think, deep down, my mom understands better than most that you've got be what you were meant to be. That's why we decided the best plan would be for her to go back to Fiji and sell spatulas, and for me to stay here in the plumbing capital of the world.

"Oh, I want to give you something," she says.

I feel my teeth grinding involuntarily. Please don't be a spatula, please don't be a spatula, please don't be a spatula...

It's not a spatula. She reaches into her purse and pulls out a small photograph—a picture of her, my dad, Emmy, and me.

"We're a family," she says, putting it in my hand. "And no matter how far apart we are, we're always together."

I don't know what to say. I try to talk, but there's a lump in my throat. Then, suddenly and without warning, it comes out.

BURRRR-RRRRRRP!

People are staring. It is the single loudest grape-flavored belch that has ever left my body. Mom is mortified.

"Phil, tell your son to say 'excuse me,'" she says. "Phil? Phil?"

But my dad doesn't hear her. He doesn't hear anything. He can't—he's in the zone! I have seen it very few times in my life, but there's no mistaking that look. His head is raised, and his lips are slightly parted, and his eyes are darting back and forth like he's reading an invisible script.

And then a hint of a smile crosses his face, and he turns to us, and speaks:

> *"I gave Romeo lots of grape soda—*
> *So much that his lips'll turn purple.*
> *And if that won't stop Juliet's kisses—*
> *I'm pretty darn sure that the burp'll."*

He did it! He did it! He rhymed the unrhymable "purple"! The whole family rushes him, and we gather there in a long, unbreakable group hug. Some of the people around us break into spontaneous applause. It's over. Phil Stringfellow's long poetry drought is over.

Wednesday, 4:10 p.m.
Thirty-two days since the Burrito Festival

I walk into the office—well, if you can call it an office. It looks more like somebody's storage closet, except there's nothing in here anybody would want to keep.

"Hi, Max," I say.

Max is sitting behind his desk, sunglasses pulled down and that tower of red hair rising up as high as ever. If he's glad to see me, it doesn't show.

"Bring me that box," he says.

Typical. No hello, no asking how I've been, no anything. I pick up the small brown box beside the door and hand it to him.

"Thanks for the plant," I say.

"Plant?"

It wasn't from him—that's what I figured. An ivy showed up at the hospital with his name on the card, but I could tell it wasn't his handwriting. My guess is it came from One-Eyed Lily Cruz. Looks like she's still trying to turn him into the one thing he's determined to never be: a decent human being.

I haven't seen Max in a month, not since he climbed out of the back of the ambulance at the Burrito Festival. A lot's changed since then. He's actually an authorized plumber now. It's almost, I don't know…respectable.

"What are you doing here?" he asks.

"Nothing," I say. "I just thought I'd drop by, see how everything is going."

"I'm living the dream," he says.

I know he's not serious, but I nod anyway.

"So…are you keeping busy?"

He puts his feet on his desk and picks up a motorcycle magazine.

"Swamped," he says.

"In that case, you probably need some help," I say.

"Nope."

I'm so stupid! Why did I do that? The last thing anyone should ever ask Max is whether he needs help.

"Right, right. I didn't mean you needed somebody to actually help you. I just thought you might want someone…," I pause because I can't believe I'm about to say this, "…to carry the toilet plunger."

Max puts down the magazine.

"You mean like a plunger caddy?"

I bite my bottom lip. Jeez, I hate that job title.

"Yeah. Like that."

He scratches his chin like he's thinking it over.

"Nope," he says at last.

"Really?"

"Really," he says.

Then he picks up his magazine again.

I guess I shouldn't be surprised. Max Bleeker works alone. Everybody knows that. I got him to break that rule once. But now I've been gone a month, and that's enough time for Max to settle back into his old ways.

I feel like I've been kicked in the stomach.

"Okay. Well, thanks anyway," I say, and I head for the door.

"Sorry, kid, but you know how it is," Max says. "I just don't happen to need a plunger caddy anymore."

"I understand," I tell him.

"But there are plenty of people who do, if you like that sort of thing. I could make some calls."

"No, I'll be all right."

"Sure you will," he says.

I open the door.

"Of course, if you know anyone who's looking for a different kind of job," he says, "one with a lot more responsibility, I might be able to use them. You know, after school, and on weekends."

I close the door.

"What kind of job are you talking about?"

Max doesn't put down the magazine. He just opens the box I brought him, takes out a small, flat object, and tosses it onto the desk. I walk back across the room.

It's laminated. Up in the top left-hand corner, there's the bright-blue P.L.U.N.G.E. insignia. But the thing that catches my attention—the thing I can't take my eyes off of—is what's printed in the very center.

"Sullivan Stringfellow, Apprentice Plumber," it says. "Bonded. Certified. Licensed to Kill."

Acknowledgments

I'll start by thanking the plumbers—all of them, everywhere—going back to the earliest builders of the aqueducts in ancient Rome. Without plumbers, the world would not be a nice place. It'd be thirsty, dirty, dry, dusty, sick, and as fragrant as the southern end of a northbound elephant. That alone makes them heroes, and it's why they inspired this book.

Others, however, played much more direct roles in creating *The Unflushables,* and I'm stunned, honored, and absolutely ecstatic that they brought their amazing gifts to this project.

From the beginning, the team at Jimmy Patterson/ Hachette welcomed me like a new member of the family. They've made this a wonderful experience. Aubrey Poole, my editor, saw possibilities in the story I never imagined. Her sense of humor is contagious, and I caught it—and if I'm very lucky, I'll never get over it. To me, she's a literary Rumpelstiltskin, taking ordinary pages and spinning them into gold.

Brandi Bowles is someone I call my agent, but only because it would take too long to explain that she is my advisor, my guide, my critic, my booster, and the well of ideas I turn to when the one in my head runs dry. She invented some of my favorite parts of this book, and put me back on course when I wandered too far from Nitro City.

While I'm at it, I'd like to send some long-overdue thanks to Mrs. Campbell, my third-grade teacher, who made me sit down and write stories when I didn't want to, and let me keep on writing when I found I couldn't stop. At the time, I didn't know she was making a real difference in my life. I know it now.

I'm also grateful to my family, and some very good friends, for giving me space when I needed it, but not so much that I ever felt alone. All I can say is that the characters on these pages would not exist without the fun and fascinating characters I have in my world.

And, of course, I owe a big thanks to the monsters out there. They make my dreams and my toilets more interesting places.

Finally, while I don't know your name, I'm grateful to you for reading this book. Writers and readers have a special connection, like travelers taking a long journey together, and I'm glad you're here and part of the adventure. Thank you, my friend.

About the Author

RON BATES is a writer, blogger, columnist, speaker, and author whose previous works include the middle-grade novels *How to Make Friends and Monsters* and *How to Survive Middle School and Monster Bots*. He began his career as a newspaper reporter, later becoming a magazine editor and a humor columnist. His writing has taken a number of different forms, including short stories, humorous poems, the comic-book series Brawn, and several short plays for children. He is an award-winning copywriter. He lives in Texas.